BIG[and BARELY ⌐AL BLONDE

FROM THE EROTIC ADVENTURES OF BRENDA NOVA

by
ALICHE KING

Limit of Liability/Disclaimer of Warranty; While the author and publisher have made their best efforts in preparing this book, they make no representations or warranties with respect to the contents of this book and specifically disclaim any implied warranties of merchantability or fitness for a particular purpose. Furthermore, this is entirely a work of fiction, though places mentioned in the book do exist, the author and publisher make no claim, direct or implied, that the events in this book have ever taken place, that the people and characters written about in the story have ever existed or their actions a representation of any person, living or dead, nor do they claim responsibility for any actions people may take regarding the content of the book, whether to seek cryptozoological life forms, mention of fictional public officials and any action persons might take regarding the content of the book, nor does it imply specific or implied knowledge of facts that are herewith publicly unknown, and disclaim any possible representation that such implied knowledge does in fact exist. No warranty may be created or extended by sales representatives or written sales materials. Neither the publisher nor the author shall be liable for any loss of profit or any other commercial damages, including but not limited to special, incidental, consequential, or other damages. Translation; If you read this book and then go to the Canadian wilderness looking for bigfoot, you can not hold us responsible for any money lost nor can you hold us responsible for any injury that may occur. However, we would be more than happy to hear about your journey, so please don't hesitate to email us at the above address.

Bigfoot And The Barely Legal Blonde/Aliche King
ISBN-13 978-1502851499
ISBN-10 1502851490

1.Cryptozoology 2.Fiction, Erotic 3.King, Aliche

Printed and/or electronically distributed in the United States of America
First Edition, October 2014

10 9 8 7 6 5 4 3 2 1

CHAPTER ONE

The girl sat in the back of the helicopter swaying and bouncing as the machine oscillated from the air currents, swells, and chop of the engine as it protested its load and proclaimed its need to be seriously overhauled. They were lucky to be far above the guys who suffered on foot or rolling in 4x4 trucks through uncivilized territory, though they would all claim the same credit for their victory. The last few hours had been painstakingly thorough, and once word came on the radio that the dogs had zeroed in on the scent of a body there were silent whispers between pairs of hardened outdoorsmen, bets if the body would be moving, silent, or covered in botflies and halfway through its natural disintegration.

The search for this girl had reached national news. People went missing in the forests of Northern Canada constantly during the seasons that school was not in session, especially early spring and summer. Panicked girlfriends and boyfriends, lovers who became separated on hiking trails, inexperienced weekenders who didn't know the first thing about outdoor hunting, survival, or navigation came in the sheriff stations and ranger posts constantly, demanding the National Guard be called out to find their sweetheart or friend who had not been seen in six hours. Almost all of the missing came walking in within a few hours, feeling sheepish and complaining about not being able to get a signal. The other kind were families missing a child, sure they had been abducted by a one armed man with a stainless steel hook they had heard about prowling these woods, an escapee from a mental asylum that had been lurking in every square acre of woodland territory in the entire English speaking world since they had heard about him in a campfire story as children themselves. The children were usually brought in by another couple whose child it had found company or playful alliance with, and the two had wandered off, eventually making their way toward one campsite leaving the other in a panic. Things rarely got serious until twenty-four hours later, which accounted for about one out of every three hundred missing person's claims. About forty percent of those turned out to be cheating lovers claiming to have gotten lost but were really at the home of another lover, another forty percent teenagers who hadn't called home, another ten percent were children who HAD gotten lost, and another seven percent were just pissed off at someone and had to take off for a few days without telling anyone, cooling off and calling in the next day.

People rarely went missing in winter, it was too cold outside to wander far from the houses or highways of the civilized world, but once the spring thaw came and kids yearned for the freedom of the outdoors, the phone started ringing and the door at the sheriff station started to swing. After twenty-four hours police went to the doors of friends and acquaintances, finding another fifty percent of those last few. After forty-eight hours, gambling husbands who had lost the family's savings and dreaded the inevitable came walking through the door to receive their due, teenagers out partying with friends came home to furious parents, and police got calls saying the children had been found playing army or pirate in the woods and camped without permission, usually at the ribbing of another child calling them cowardly for having to report in to their mothers.

Then there were the actual missing people. These were the ones who became news, the ones who really WERE lost, the ones who had gotten disoriented or injured far, far from where anybody knew where they were, the only people noticing their absence being co-workers who noticed they hadn't been at work without calling or friends and relatives who would have been reported to by now. After three days, the call went out, and the search parties and posses blew the dust off of their binoculars, rounded up their dogs, and changed the spark plugs in the helicopter. After seventy-two hours, it was official. All local resources had been exhausted, all known associates of the missing had been contacted, and the word went out. The news agencies were notified and depending on the character of the missing decided if they were newsworthy. Elderly retirees not seen in days were definitely newsworthy. Old people rarely went missing, and unless suffering from Alzheimer's or other debilitating illness of the mind, were smart enough to stay put and out of the way of the fast moving world. Illegal aliens were never newsworthy unless wanted for other crimes since it was impossible to track down all of their possible locations, and their families were reticent to give any other information other than the fact that they were missing, plus if they were arrested in another part of the territory they were likely to give a false name due to the fact that they carried no identification.

Children were also newsworthy since it raised awareness in the neighborhoods of sexual predators and other evil phantoms that were the greatest real fear for parents and sold countless bars of soap, cereal boxes, and cans of underarm deodorant for sponsors of the news stations. Everyone followed missing children stories like everyone went to the races to see cars crash. There is in innate morbid curiosity in us that the fear of a missing child puts that great evil at the front of, as the abuse, execution, and dissection of a young child is the farthest thing from our desires, the exact polar opposite of the happiness we so desperately seek, and nothing, NOTHING, could be worse than the abduction and death of our children, not even our OWN deaths, so we follow with clenched teeth, waiting for the word that will either send sighs of relief to thousand of parents clutching their children tight, locking their windows at night and calling their kids in from play before the sun sets, or morosely paying homage to the candlelight vigils that come when the story has a far less favorable outcome. The other newsworthy missing people are wanted criminals, but those are a dime a dozen and never looking their best in their mug shots, so we wish for their capture and to never have to meet them face to face.

There is one group of missing people who warrant more press and publicity than almost all others combined, and with good reason. These are the pretty girls who go missing, and barely a week goes by that some alluring teenager isn't national news in one form or another, whether suspected of having been abducted, fleeing across state lines with a boyfriend, or having simply vanished. The better looking they are, the more news stations pick up on it, and within a matter of hours, a simple missing persons report can be national news. The more pictures that are available, the easier and greater the story spreads. Pretty girls are almost always popular in their schools, and photos of them in cheerleading outfits, smiling in summer clothes with their hair tumbling about them and surrounded by friends are produced by the hundreds by friends and admirers who want to do their part to bring their sweet object of affection, whether reciprocated or not, home.

Emily was one of those girls. She had been national news since she had been reported missing in the North Canadian wilderness almost four weeks ago, and now, against much greater odds, she was coming home. She was an anomaly for a missing person, and speculation ran amongst the rescue workers and search parties about what had happened to her. It wasn't that she was injured, in fact, they couldn't find a mark on her except for a handful of bruises that convinced the rescue workers that she had been handled very roughly, but they were inconsistent with the scratches and scrapes found on people who had survived outdoors from imminent and constant contact with rocks, trees, insect bites, and sleeping on the forest floor. In fact, she was in remarkably good shape for someone who had been missing in the Northern Canadian woods for the last four weeks. They felt lucky to have found her alive at all, and the first responders who had been on the case since she had first been reported missing were already swelling with pride at having found her in one piece.

Their minds were swimming with the thoughts of their faces on television as they described the battle against nature and their refusal to give up until they found her. They tried to keep from smiling as they thought about the attention they would get from the local women as they humbly accepted their kisses and adoration at their bravery and selflessness. They played over and over again, like a record stuck on the best part of a song, the welcome their wives and girlfriends would give them when they arrived home, loaded with apologies at having nagged them for spending so much time looking for a girl who wasn't their problem, and the subservient nature they would display in bed that night knowing that their husbands could have any woman in the district that night, married or not, owing to their new fame as heroes and humanitarians. After all, one man could not claim credit where others had not, it was a team effort, and even those who were miles away and nowhere near her point of discovery took up the cry, "WE'VE FOUND HER!" and as part of the team, were all allowed equal credit.

"Careful, dammit! Just fly this thing straight and get us home. She's not bleeding to death, just take it easy." Even though the searchers were successful and thrilled at finding the girl alive, they were still stressed from lack of sleep and exhaustion that a search this long brings. Several facts contributed to their refusal to call off the search. First of all, there were signs of a struggle where she had gone missing from, and the boyfriend who had been on the scene had been cleared of suspicion, at least to a minimal amount. Second, no other story made sense, and they had several witnesses who placed her at the scene of abduction, the pilot who dropped them off, the convenience store clerk who sold them liquor and food, so she was confirmed to be seen leaving for the woods with camping gear and a canoe, leaving no other story except to look for an abductor, who was their other reason to search. Third, she was a pretty girl, and pretty girls are good press. Had she not been found and skeletal remains discovered later in the year or next season, her picture would return to the front pages of newspapers and television and Internet news stations, and the blame for not finding her placed on the ennui of the people who were now bringing her home. Normally after four weeks they would be bringing home black plastic garbage bags filled with remains dragged out of the river or a gurney with a white sheet wrapping a decaying camper head to toe under locking straps.

This girl wasn't dead though...this girl had only been ASSUMED dead, having been missing for four weeks in the wilderness. Somehow, this girl had stayed warm, found fresh water, eaten enough of and the right kinds of food, kept her sanity, found shelter, and beaten the odds. When they found her, she was in her oversized blue flannel shirt, a pair of hiking boots on her feet, and nothing else. Right away the workers were doing their best to remain gentlemen, but their eyes gave away their real thoughts. Her legs were long and shapely, and the wind or her movements made the flannel shirt rise up in the back giving the men a glimpse of her naked ass, and no matter how mature you were trying to be, if you were a man, it was nearly impossible to look away. The flannel only had the bottom two buttons done, so her breasts hugged her hair in between them as if reticent to let go, and they all ran up to her offering coats and parkas, but in reality they all were vying for her favor in a ritual as old as time. It also gave them a chance to get up close and look at her breasts poking through the shirt and see her ass dying to be held as if it were a Christmas morning teddy bear.

When the report initially came in, the hiker whom she had gone into the lakes with had lost her and was panicked with fear. They wanted to go on a canoeing adventure, and though they both had plenty of wilderness experience they became separated during a stop near a waterfall, and he was convinced she had been abducted.

"We got a guy here, says his girlfriend was on a camping trip with him, they hitched up the boats to camp for the night, but at some point just before sunrise, she went out of sight. The guy thought she was just answerin' nature, but after twenty minutes or so, she didn't answer his calls. He shouted and fired off a few rounds, but there was no sign of her. He said he had been passed out drunk the night before, so wasn't sure exactly what time she went missing. He spent the day screaming her name and stompin' around the woods, so any tracks that might have been left are more than likely erased. It wasn't until about noon the next day he was able to get to a rangers station to get the call in. "

They all heard the call over the radio. Lost campers were as common as pinecones around here, and there was a procedure that they had to follow. They sent up a ranger experienced in these matters to look at the point where she was last seen, and an investigative officer interviewed the person claiming to be the last to see her. About one time in ten thousand, the person being interviewed skinned the missing person and wrapped chains around their remains, tossing the bloody mess into the nearest deep water. The investigators knew what kind of questions to ask and what to look for to see if the suspect could have done such a thing, but in this case it hadn't seemed to be so.

The rescue workers and volunteer search parties came in shifts, and usually it never took more than one shift to bring the person home. A few flares shot off and a run or two with an airplane or helicopter was usually enough to spot anyone lost for a day or two. It was difficult to get more than a few miles on foot, so a search radius was easy to map out. Even though it was easy enough to get disoriented in the woods, once you heard that plane engine you came running out of whatever hole you had made for yourself and flagged it down, problem solved. If, after the fifth day the missing person STILL hadn't shown up, they started looking a little harder at the last person to see them. NOW they were starting to think that that missing person was BURIED somewhere in that radius, and they brought out the dogs. Oh, they TOLD everyone that they were searching for the PERSON, and the news teams and reporters talk about the dogs searching for the scent of the person, but what these dogs were REALLY trained to do was to sniff out BODIES. The dogs were cute and couldn't talk, so they showed the hounds on the news, along with a picture of the missing, and that's when the search party turned into a national story.

The girl who was missing, Emily Wrennington, was a second year college student with giant blue doll eyes, dark blonde wavy hair, that thick, heavy hair that wouldn't style no matter what, but fell about her shoulders and the curves of her breasts outlining them and curling at the bottom so her hair almost looked like it was supporting her tits from below. Her teeth were white and perfect, and her eyes smiled in her picture along with her mouth. You knew she was the type of girl who smiled for real, because when she had her picture taken there were six of her friends waiting behind the camera to go

12

out to get coffee with her, so her smile was genuine. It must have affected the people of the area deeply, because two hundred locals turned up to join her search party. Usually they could count on about ten, but usually the person missing was a local logger who had gotten drunk and wandered away from his nagging wife at a bar and not returned home. Those guys were usually found at a girlfriend's house or a bar outside the city limits with a lawless community and enough meth labs to keep everyone awake for a few years.

Emily wasn't the type to go missing or run off with a guy. She was the kind of girl who cleaned her room before leaving the house every day, woke up extra early to shower and eat a healthy breakfast, ironed her clothes so that they fit her perfectly, and her bra and panties were always white as snow. She wasn't the type to go off with some guy; she had no issues with her roommates or her parents (things other girls blame for their disappearances), and had no money or drug problems. The only inconsistent thing in her life was her weight, which fluctuated between curvy and 'just got back from Thanksgiving holiday'. It was never an issue with her or a source of anxiety, and if she put on a few extra pounds she carried it with charm and grace without ever seeming to notice, even if others did. She was bright, pretty, well liked around school, and if there were a lumberjack or an Esquimaux in her life, well, her friends would have known about it. There was a lot about her disappearance that just didn't make sense, and there was a lot about her reappearance that didn't make sense EITHER.

The picture of her on the television made about every single guy in the county search the areas around his house. Everyone wanted to be the hero, everyone wanted to be the guy to walk into town, the girl nestled in his arms as he carried her out of the woods and back to civilization, the girl showing her undying gratification to him with every curve of her body, his for life for saving HERS, and his picture in the paper and on the news. In case you missed our earlier broadcast, here she is in her swimsuit, here she is in her cheerleading outfit, here she is in her prom dress, every picture slightly photoshopped by a crafty station manager to make her breasts just a little bit larger.

The couple had been canoeing in Northern Quebec by Pointe Louis XIV, then hitched a ride from a pilot who told them about the beautiful coastline and scenic wildlife to be found over Hudson Bay at a point known as Inukjuak, where he was dropping off medicine and supplies for the fisheries located on the lake. They were going to meet the same pilot in three days, and they made sure to get contact numbers from the pilot and the friend of a friend up at Inukjuak point, and give those numbers to friends who would notice their absence and report it if they went unheard from. It seemed like the ideal romantic getaway, only after they had rowed their canoe up the coast and camped for the first night, Emily suddenly disappeared. After a long and exhaustive search by the local peacekeeper and the search posse they gathered up, grumblings about what happened were heard amongst the local men, but they refused to talk about what they thought. One of the investigators was part Chehalis Indian, and he heard a word he recognized being muttered by the local loggers who were also Native Canadian.

The word was 'Saskehavas'.

"Was there anything else strange, anything at all you can think of that coincided with her disappearance, no matter how small or strange? Something you might think is insignificant might be the clue we need to put this together."

The investigators had asked him time and time again about the night she disappeared. He had told them about the blood that he saw, but it was so contaminated from the dirt it was scattered on it was impossible to test a sample for any kind of identifying features. The terrified kid took a drag of his cigarette and seemed to focus for a minute, and the rangers all leaned in close to him.

"Well, you all might think I'm crazy, yeah? But the one thing I did not want to say is during the night, after we got totally drunk and I was pretty much passed out, I could swear I heard wolves growling and barking and fighting outside my tent. I know wolves don't attack people so I thought they were just stray coyote fighting over leftover food we had sitting out, or some meat had fallen on the campfire and they were fishing it out and getting burned but I never for a minute thought that they were after Emily, who I thought was asleep next to me. But then I heard the dogs cry like they were being hurt, and I could swear I saw a PERSON outside of my tent, but I saw it was all covered with fur so I knew it was just a bear on his hind legs, and the coyote were fighting with the bear. Shit like that happens out in the wilderness, and I wanted to see it, but I was too drunk and didn't want either the bear or the coyote or the wolves or WHATEVER coming back for me or the food they know campers keep in their tents. I must have passed right back out because next thing I knew it was morning, Emily was gone, and I went outside and there was some blood and the place was wrecked, so I spent half the day screaming her name until I got scared and came into town and told the sheriff what happened."

They told the kid not to leave town, but it didn't seem to ANYONE that he was the kind of kid to rape and kill a girl, or get in a fight and accidentally bang her head against a rock. No, he was a good kid and had a crush on Emily for years, so everyone was pretty sure he wasn't hiding a body anywhere. His family had lived in Northern Canada for three generations, so he had known many of the people investigating her disappearance, rangers and sheriffs, since birth. He was not only mortified at the fact that he had lost her, but also because during questioning he was searched and a box of condoms fell out of his pack right in front of her father.

The days turned into weeks, and they called off the air and dog searches. Now they were dragging chains along the bottom of the lake and diving in any rivers close to their campsite. The radius of the search expanded daily, and the rescue effort was turning into a search for remains. The survival rate dropped to less than five percent after the seventh day for a semi skilled outdoorsperson alone in the Canadian wilderness. Water was easy enough to find, but the real enemy was the cold. A fire wasn't a difficult thing to get started, but keeping it going meant you had to wake up every hour to feed the flames with wood, and after even a few sleepless nights like this your body would soon shut down. Combine this with bitter cold, hunger, swarms of bugs crawling over you all night driving you crazy, disorientation, fear, exhaustion, and less than hygienic facilities, and the survival factor for more than fifteen days dwindled to about two percent. In winter, that figure was as close to zero as could be.

However, Canadian Mounties are known for their resilience and tact, and the search party decided to do a sweep of the area north of the bay in case the current washed her body up along the lakeside. Once the dogs locked on to a scent they decided to go up by helicopter, and that's when they found her. One of the rangers saw a little white dot along the shoreline, and as they approached, he saw it dart into the forest. They landed as quickly as they could, and followed what they were sure was a person into the woods. Quickly catching up with her, they had to tackle and carry the girl, dressed only in her flannel shirt, screaming and kicking back to the helicopter.

Once they had her secured, they figured she was just in a state of shock. Everyone else they had rescued covered them with thanks and hugs, and was more than thrilled to be going back to civilization, except for the few teenage lovers they had to practically separate with a crowbar. This one was fighting them every step of the way, as if she were being hauled off to jail.

"We're RANGERS!" They yelled at her, trying to calm her down. "We're here to take you HOME!" At which point she collapsed, sobbing into their arms.

"BUT I DON'T WANT TO GO HOME!" she cried, gasping for breath. She made no attempt to be modest, and her armpits, pussy, and legs showed a four-week growth of hair she made no attempt to hide. Her fingernails, toenails, hair and teeth seemed to have taken on a wild, savage look, and she gave off the distinct odor that animals have at the zoo or on the farm. The smell wasn't of rotten meat, but more like old blood, wet wood, dry earth. For her to transform from a preppy college student to this animal like being in a few weeks must have been due to a seriously traumatic event, or so the rangers thought. They talked about going back to look for her abductor, at which point she flew into another rage.

"THERE'S NO ONE UP HERE!!!" She screamed, at which point the rescue workers all looked at one another.

"Stockholm syndrome. That's where the kidnap victims identify with their captors, and become friends with them. Sometimes they don't even want to be rescued. I'm sure that's what happened to this little lady here, but we got to go and get him. We can't have people getting kidnapped in the middle of the woods."

"Who was it that took you, young lady?" They all looked at her for a response, but she just stared out the window. "Who took care of you and fed you? Did they have a cabin out in the woods?" Again she just stared out the window, not making a sound. "Were they white men? Were they native Canadians?"

"HAH!" She suddenly burst out. They all turned to look at her, and with her face pressed up against the window; they could barely hear her whisper,

"Yeah, they were native, all right."

CHAPTER TWO

"So Brenda, do you understand why it's important to keep the current capital gains tax at the level it is now? I know it's an all time high, but the revenue generated will help pay for schools and roads."

"And those all expense paid trips to Europe so you can frolic with your French girlfriend at the taxpayers' expense?" Brenda was buttoning up her silk blouse, and couldn't help but to admire her own breasts and how great they looked in the white lace bra she just bought to show them off in. She never saw clothes as covering, she saw them as more like wrapping paper, and the better wrapped the gifts underneath, the more she could get for them. In this case, she asked Senator Jenesson if she could have priority access to Federal Hearings and NSA security clearance if she could get the jackass she was with now, Senator McFarlan, to drop his bid for re-election. Of course, a few nights of pleasure with that amazing body would be thrown in for good measure, but that was understood.

"That's the third time you've made an accusation at me, Miss Nova. I thought we were getting to be friends. I was hoping to see you on the press security clearance sheet for next term." Senator McFarlan was still young enough to be thought of as attractive, but he made the mistake of thinking women were attracted to HIM, not his money or title. Brenda was attracted to neither, and that veiled threat he just blurted out made it all that more fun to stick the knife in his small dick, couldn't make a girl come with a vibrator, premature ejaculating body.

"There won't be a next term, Senator. You see, I just got back from Paris where I interviewed the nineteen year old girl you just dumped, and she HATES your lying ass. I guess you promised to bring her to the States to study dance, but you got cold feet and left her a check for three thousand Francs and a goodbye letter after she quit nursing school for you. It's all on video, care to see? Maybe later. Plus, I've got one of the guys in your office, I won't name names, but HE'S got a little report on you taking out loans from a bank YOU bailed out using taxpayer money. That's not the only law broken here, the collateral on those loans is valuable art from a non profit company YOU raised funds for, and the SAME artwork is used as collateral on at LEAST seven loans totaling over twenty million dollars, and I'll bet it all that you couldn't come up with ONE payment receipt for those loans, am I right? So those loans are actually laundered and deposited into your accounts as "re-election campaign funds", and they're never repaid, and THAT'S illegal too. And finally, that little dance I just performed on your dick? That's already in the hands of some very reliable friends who are just DYING to see your face right now. OOPS! THERE THEY ARE! SAY HI GUYS!" Brenda turned her clutch purse so that the senator could see the camera lens, and smiled as he slumped into the seat as he mentally murdered her.

"You see senator, I WILL be on the press security clearance list, it's just that YOU won't be senator anymore. This isn't anywhere NEAR the total amount of dirt that's been dug up on you. You have been a very, VERY bad boy, and I'm afraid your time in the seat of power is up. You are going to announce your withdrawal from your re-election bid citing health and family issues, no one will ask any questions about those, but you will still get your full pension, enough to live comfortably on. All of the taxpayer money and non-repayable loans you procured however will be transferred from your offshore account to the Federal Appropriations Committee, with the explanation that it was erroneously deposited into your campaign accounts. You have enough loyalty in your old friends that they know what's up and will cover for you. This is your only option, of course, unless you'd prefer JAIL, senator."

The senator sat there with his mouth open. In the space of two minutes, he had gone from a multimillionaire playboy with a Rolodex full of jet setting world leader golf buddies, to a middle class retiree with a state pension. In one fell swoop the yachts, the houses in Monaco, the private jet, and the harem of women were all gone, and there was nothing he could do about it. Nothing except.....

"All right, how much do you want?" Everyone had a price, and he was hoping this bitch could be bought, blackmailed, silenced, or killed, but first, he had to find out who was pulling her strings. His hopes ran high for a second, as she turned and looked at him with a smile, but that quickly faded as she moved closer and closer, bending over and revealing those perfect breasts that had been in his mouth only five minutes ago.

"Honey, right now you couldn't afford the upgrade to first class to fly home. There's nothing you have that I want. I've already taken it all. So why don't you take that bullshit about schools and potholes you tell your constituents every time there's a tax increase, along with the bullshit you tried to sell me, and try to sell it to your wife and kids, who are probably going to disown you after they find out you're fucking broke, because I know assholes like you, and the ONLY reason anyone in your family even PRETENDS to like you is because they're counting the minutes until you DIE. Then you can see how much they love you when they dance on your grave with the money you've left them, only there is none, so I guess you'll die in a state home for the elderly, choking on your mush and smelling your overflowing colostomy bag."

Brenda packed up the rest of her things and left the senator to his thoughts. She lived for days like this. If the people of the world knew how much world politics were influenced and decided by women and their pussies, men wouldn't be swinging their dicks around thinking they're such hot shit. Unfortunately, this wasn't the case everywhere and she made it her mission to change that. In many parts of the world, women were still seen as possessions, like cattle to be traded, beaten, and sold. Still, she felt satisfied that she was doing as much as she could. Most of the dirty money she received a cut of in bribes or kickbacks she put into her own non-profit, a shelter and rehabilitation home for girls and women who had been victims of the international sex trade. This she kept as quiet as possible, because rescuing and giving a home to hundreds of former prostitutes had robbed the crime syndicates, fascist dictators, tribal chiefs, and pimp scumbags of the world of millions of dollars, and they wouldn't hesitate for a minute to take out whoever was taking away their assets.

This was something she had given a lot of thought to. To stop the international sex trade, you had to eliminate demand for the product, which was sex. Well, that was never going to happen, but she reasoned that men pay for sex partially because they can't get it any other way, and partially because the kind of sex they wanted, be it fantasy, BDSM, watersports, or whatever, their current partner wasn't into. She figured if the stigma of casual sex could be removed from society, there wouldn't be a need for sexual enslavement, because everyone would act like grownups for once and sex would be as easy as asking someone out to the movies. Girls wouldn't be called sluts for engaging in healthy sex the way men aren't, and people would lose their hang ups about it. The sad thing is, EVERYONE wants a healthy sex life. It's just people who no longer feel sexually attractive or think that abstaining makes you a better person who are the problem, and that's why it has to be sold by criminals, because the one thing we desire almost daily, some more than others, is ILLEGAL TO BUY. Birth control was easy enough, and there were advances on the eradication of STD's every day, plus every adult should know about proper condom use, and society was become less and less controlled by religious zealots, who we were finding out to be child molesting homosexuals and perverts anyway. Those reasons alone should take us out of the sexual repression of the 1800's, but not much had changed, in the eyes of society anyway.

This was the other way she tried to make the world a better place. Men wouldn't be so uptight and women wouldn't be so catty and competitive if people were relaxed about sex. It was as necessary as food and water, and your body insisted you needed it from puberty until the day you died. So why did people get arrested for following their natural instincts and patronize prostitutes when they couldn't get it somewhere else? That's how people on top stay in power. She knew the game of power very well, and the people on top were the most depraved sexual deviants, but they had the ability to arrest everyone else for following the SAME instincts. It was a dirty power play, and she was bound and determined to expose the guilty some day. For now, she had to use sex as her favorite pastime, and share with those who deserved her affections, as well as seducing those who deserved punishment. If only she could teach all women of the world the power they wield between their legs, and how to get men to obey using that power, she could make the world a unified, happy, war and starvation free sexual playground. Well, that's what she loved to tell herself anyway, and the thought of sex shops as ubiquitous as fast food restaurants and the finding of sex partners as easy as dialing the phone made her lips wet with pleasure.

Those damned churches though... She got angry every time she thought about them. Those high and mighty rabbis, clergymen, priests, elders, all of those assholes who brought the wrath of whatever god they prayed to down on their people, they were the ones who kept the world in the dark ages. It wouldn't be so bad if these men were as chaste as they proclaimed to be, but Brenda knew that those bastards were the ones who patronized the brothels and hookers of the world the most! Not only that, but they used their power over their congregation to seduce the ones they found attractive, or weasel money out of the wealthiest ones. Two years ago she had done a story posing as a new parishioner at a church, synagogue, and temple, and after acting stupid and impressed at the influence of the holy man in charge, they each took a try at offering her immortal soul a place of reverence if she just performed the ancient and holy act of fellatio on them. The only exception was the priest, whom she discovered after leaving a camera in the rectory that he preferred young boys. He now spent his time on his knees in San Quentin.

Being a reporter held more weight than people could possibly imagine. In ancient times, the person with the mightiest army was king. Later on, the wealthiest landowner was king. More recently, whoever held the latest technology was king. But now, the people who had the power over information and the ability to sway public opinion held almost ALL of the chips, and she was one of the best-loved reporters on the scene. She had met, interviewed, fucked, blown, jacked off, been fondled by, and performed stripteases and lesbian fuck fests for more congressmen, business giants, movie stars, foreign diplomats, drug lords, royalty, rock musicians, and media moguls than a grade a porn star, and she kept them all in her back pocket.

She never saw sex as an emotional jewelry box, only to be opened by the people with the charm to crack the code. No, that was for girls who got dumped and left on the roadside, crying about how they were promised the world by some asshole who left them with runny mascara and a shitty reputation. For Brenda, it was more of a meeting of the superpowers, and AFTER she got what SHE wanted, an interview, access to a press conference, inside information (which she tactfully went to press with at the EXACT minute it was exposed to the world, giving her an edge on her competition but never ruining the trust her informant put into her), or an invite to an earth changing event, she made sure to reward those who took care of her by sharing what she felt was a gift to the world, and something every man wanted. It wasn't just pussy, EVERY girl had a pussy, and they weren't hard to get. What men wanted was simply reassurance that they were doing the right thing. Men in power were ALWAYS second guessing themselves, and no one, not their WIVES, not their generals, vice presidents, NO ONE, made them feel that they were doing the right thing for the millions of people affected by their decisions.

Brenda knew EXACTLY which people were making WHAT decisions that they were stressed about, found them at the right time, and let them know that they were doing the right thing. She had a special knack for it, and the body she had grown up with was the reward that all men sought. Who was she to keep it to herself? If someone made a decision, a HARD decision, that made the world a better place, they usually came home to a wife who asked them why they never paid attention to them anymore, why they were drinking so much, and they also had a roomful of underlings ready to jump ship if things turned out wrong, and they knew it and it gave them ulcers. But the one thing that made them smile was their press secretary going, "Brenda Nova is asking to schedule an interview. She can be here in six hours." The smile that came over their faces was all the reward they wanted, because they knew that the privacy of that interview would include delights and affection that would make the whole wicked world slip away. Every once in awhile she would take down an asshole like Senator McFarlan just to make sure everyone remembered the power she held, and most were in awe. It was the life she had wanted for herself since she was thirteen, and at just twenty-four, she had more adventures around the world than anyone else she knew. There was a consistent stream of news worldwide, and she was able to select between three or four assignments happening simultaneously at different points on the globe. Life was good.

She arrived home to her Los Angeles loft on downtown's west side and checked her messages. She had been gone only twenty four hours, but there were at least thirty messages on her personal number, and her Facebook and twitter accounts had so many incoming letters she finally had to write up a standard reply that was sent to everyone who wrote; "Hi and thanks for taking the time to write. Unfortunately, I can't answer all of my messages personally, but I want you to know I read almost all of my messages and love you dearly for sending them.... If there's something REALLY important, please contact the editorial staff at the Los Angeles Media Center, and they'll get the message to me depending on the level of importance, but please don't tie up the lines there with party invites and date requests. As flattered as I am by your invitations, someone could be in danger or need real help and not be able to get through at the newspaper because the lines are tied up. You're a DARLING to be so understanding, and I look forward to when we see each other face.... to .....face."

She constantly checked her messages on her smartphone while on assignment but almost never answered it, partially because she had the phone off when speaking to a VIP, and partially because she didn't want her phone to ring while she was getting her pussy licked, or was in the middle of giving a royal rim job to one of Her Majesty's Royal next- in – lines. There were about eighty of those; they had that lineage traced for eight hundred years. Brenda had personally fucked about twenty five of them, some so close to the crown they could almost touch it, and all it would take was one plane crash or one flu epidemic to wipe out those that stood before them. However, the royal family wasn't as scandalous as most other people in power were, no matter what people thought. Sure, their ancestors were some of the most violent and predatory monarchs in history, but these days, they were a lovely group, and Brenda had been welcome at every royal function for the last three years. She rarely took them up on it unless she was already in England. The paper she worked at had no qualms about sending her at a moments' notice. Even though they had staff reporters on the scene already, Brenda had that special gift of getting pictures, interviews, and quotes that were exclusive to her.

The Los Angeles Media Center also licensed out her stories to dozens of internet news agencies, so her text and videos were major sources of income for the media company that owned newspapers and a dozen internet news outlets, and the old man who ran the whole thing was treated to a special visit from Brenda at least once a month. She wouldn't leave until the old man was grinning from ear to ear. Share your blessings with the world, and the world will love you for it. She wished everyone thought the same.

She got undressed, washed, and listened to the rest of her messages while getting ready to take a serious eight-hour nap. The usual party invites, ex boyfriends, ex girlfriends, and possible employers filled up most of her messages, and she sat and listened closely to a few at the end that she rewound to hear again. She brushed her dark chestnut streaked hair, released her boobs from what felt like a satin iron maiden, and stroked them as they popped out and felt her nipples brush against the silk of her night blouse. She was diminutive, a little over 5'3, but with platform heels she was almost 5'10. She had the 'hips of doom' they called them at the office, and you could hear the jungle drums as she walked by. Every guy at the office, and most of the girls stopped to watch her walk, and it was an art form in itself. Her father taught her how to walk like a lady, always heel to toe, always with her feet in a straight line, NEVER side by side. Your thighs had to cross one in front of the other, as a proper lady should. Of course, as soon as her hips developed, this 'elegant walk' of a young lady turned into the strut of a vixen, and even the girls at her high school were jealous. They had hips and boobs too, so why were all the guys watching Brenda all the time?

Her stomach was as flat as she could keep it, and this wasn't very much or very often. Girdles were her best friends, because there was NO WAY she was going to miss out on the sumptuous feasts they served at the palatial gatherings she was invited to. She tried as best she could to limit her servings, but even taking one bite of each delicacy was a full three-course meal. The last one she went to served sorbet and custard ice as an appetizer, followed by soybeans braised in goat's butter. The first course was vegetables, broccoli and shitake mushrooms broiled in olive oil and sugarcane with mint sprigs and parsnip garnish, and she tried to fill up on the veggies as much as possible, but then the second course came...Duck a l'orange with oysters on the half shell and steamed endives, something she absolutely couldn't resist, so she filled up on that, knowing nothing could be better.

After everyone had a bit of time to digest and a glass of wine, then they brought out the big guns, lobster bisque soup with filet mignon and béarnaise sauce, along with artichoke heart fettuccini alfredo. This was too much for her to take, and she once again dove in, eating everything, promising herself not to eat again for the rest of the month. She even said a prayer, asking the universe not to bring out any more delicious food, but the universe wasn't listening. After the plates were cleared and another fifteen minutes went by, giant silver serving plates were passed around the tables so that everyone could be served at the same time, and when they were opened, giant billowing clouds of steam rose to the ceiling with the wonderful fragrance of lemon and fish cooked to perfection. The salmon steaks were wild Alaskan, lightly peppered with cinnamon and blackened on the skin to give the right crunch and let the flavor from the pinkish orange flesh come through.

Requests from the universe weren't enough, now she was trying to bargain with the devil for her soul. "You can have my soul", she though jokingly, "If I can eat all this and not gain an ounce, ok?" She felt that was good enough, and laughing to herself, dove in. Finally, they brought out buttermilk cream on sweetened bread, which you poured together and scooped up with sliced strawberries. Well this was all natural, so it was okay, right? Right. After finishing that off, she was too full to do anything, too stuffed full of food to do her interview, and MUCH too tired to fuck. She was a guest in the embassy for the night, and she knew the Shah would be around in the morning, so she politely excused herself from the festivities, and after a round of protests from her Arabian friends, she went to her room to digest her meal like an anaconda that had just swallowed a goat.

That was just two nights ago, and she hadn't kept her promise not to eat afterwards, which made her mad at herself. This was her only weakness, and it was sure to destroy her, she thought giggling. She looked at herself in the mirror, and thought there was no way she could keep her shape if she kept going to these embassy dinner parties, so she made a mental note to limit these to once every two weeks. She could suck in her belly standing up, but when she sat down, her body betrayed her secret desire for eating. It wasn't a disorder, well, not THAT much, I mean, EVERY girl likes to watch her calorie intake, right? When she sat on the bed, the little rolls above her waist made her look in the mirror and give out a "HMPH!" before putting her flannel pajama bottoms on. She was so intent on her figure that she only caught the last few words of a message, but she rewound it and played it again.

'Hey Bren, it's Stewart Black Sky, from Canada.... You did a piece on the plight of the Native Canadians a few years ago, remember? Well, I have a story you might be interested in. A girl was just rescued from being in the wilderness for about a month. She couldn't have survived on her own, and she won't talk about who either helped her or kidnapped her. We think it might be Stockholm syndrome, but we're not sure. She was found almost naked in the middle of the forest, and at first she didn't even want to be rescued. We think if you came and talked to her, you might be able to find out where she's been.

There's one other thing. Most of the evidence was destroyed by search parties, but we caught a few of the searchers trying to erase what looked like tracks in the dirt near where she went missing. I didn't get a good look at them, but I speak enough of the native tongue that I could hear what they were saying. I really only caught one word, but the word I heard was "Saskehavas", a word that translates to "Sasquatch".

"Brenda, these guys think she was kidnapped and kept hostage by a Bigfoot."

CHAPTER THREE

"But you've GOT to let me go to Canada!" Brenda was whining, something she HATED to do, but her boss wanted her on a more 'prestigious' assignment. There was a summit meeting that included peace talks for the disputed islands between Japan, China, and Taiwan, and Brenda's boss knew how much the Japanese dignitaries adored her. She would have been more than happy to go, but she had done that trip a dozen times already in the last year, and she hadn't been to the Canadian wilderness in several years. It was her way of getting her boss to pay for a relaxing vacation, and he knew it.

Stories like this were a journalists' dream, because there was such a wide margin of accountability that they could make up whatever they wanted to and no one would believe the person who originally told the story. Would you believe someone who was yelling, "NO! It wasn't like that at ALL! The aliens were trying to tell me that I had to convince the leaders of the world to stop nuclear testing, or we would be invaded, NOT that we would be invaded by aliens with nuclear weapons! DON'T YOU SEE THE DIFFERENCE!?!?" Even if the news channels ran the controversy, people were just as apt to tune in and laugh at the poor victim, sure they were just out of their minds, and the reporter could print whatever the hell they wanted, saying that was the original story, and the victim was just crazy and rambling.

The reason Brenda wanted this story was not only for the week in the Canadian mountains, but because she was wired a picture of the girl who was found. She was an awesome beauty, gorgeous flowing dishwater blonde hair, eighteen year old ass and hips, full, bee stung lips that were only upstaged by her silky green eyes. Brenda almost blushed looking at her, finally noticing that people were speaking to her and she hadn't said a word, not even realizing she was being spoken to. She put the photo down and looked at Mel, her boss, and started in on an old and practiced speech.

"Mel, you know as well as I do that anyone can cover the summit conference. You just want to send me because you think I might get privileged information from the Japanese, but you know in meetings like this there are spies everywhere, so no one will be talking, and I'll be on my knees just for the fun of it. Plus, both the Chinese and the Japanese think of women as second-class citizens, and even though they LOVE me, send someone else. This story in the Canadian wilderness has got everything- a victim who probably had a sexual relationship with her abductor, and from what I can tell, it was a mutually beneficial relationship. She's also insanely gorgeous, so I'll get it on every North American news channel that isn't already covering it. I'll bring Brian As my video/ camera guy, and we'll make her look like a porn star in heat. "

Brian was her favorite travelling tech/camera/audio/ bodyguard/cook/drinking buddy, and they rarely had a less than adventurous time together. He was brave enough to protect her from unscrupulous mafia gangsters, but let her leash go enough not to interfere if she was seducing a member of the Swiss royal family under investigation. He always knew where to find her in the morning, and more times than she could count he rescued her from the clutches of an evil drug lord or fascist dictator in the nick of time. He was also a former rock star and pornographer, so his knowledge in the high tech world of audio and video was unsurpassed. He had a good amount of his own connections, so together they were a great team. As an added bonus, once in awhile, on an assignment far from home, in a hotel bored out of their minds, he knew just how to come on to her, and he picked up on her signal to leave it alone, come on slowly, or use her body like his own personal fuck toy, and he could switch to the gear she wanted in the blink of an eye. He never got possessive or jealous except when she needed him to get her out of trouble, and if a guy ever made her feel blue he was there with popcorn, a foot massage, and a chick movie, which she KNEW he hated, but still, there he was, to make everything all better. If she could pick one guy to stay with forever, it would be him. Every girl should have a Brian, she always thought to herself.

"Listen, no one cares about these "in search of" stories anymore. No one has caught a U.F.O., the Loch Ness Monster, found Atlantis, hordes of Nazi gold, and I'm sure there's a small percentage of the population that will always want to read stories like these, but right now, there are more important things going on." Mel was standing his ground, but Brenda started to think, "What if this horny old bastard is just trying to get me to convince him? He KNOWS I'm right, and ANYONE could cover the summit, but does he want me to talk him into it? That sneaky fucker!" She couldn't help laughing as Mel stood there with his arms crossed, looking at her as if spaghetti was shooting out of her ears.

"Okay, boss. You win. I'll do the conference. You're right. No one wants to hear about Canada except during hockey season. Get my travel plans for the summit together, but I still want Brian on crew, ok? But just remember, things like the coelacanth, the Higgs boson 'God Particle', even the city of Troy were all thought to be non existent on Earth until somebody went out and found them."

Mel looked at her for a second with his mouth open. He had NEVER heard her give up so easily on something, and he had no idea what to say. With her, any rules he made were for everyone else, but with her, they were "suggestions".

"Well, uh......you see, Brenda, if you go to the summit, I think it would look great to have you, um, representing the company, and, um...... I know everyone would want to see you,....and, um......you can still go with Brian, ok?" He wasn't sure what to say at that point. He HAD wanted her to 'talk him into it', but her refusal to do so had left him wondering what to do. He also had no idea what the fuck a coelacanth was either, but didn't want to admit it. She didn't sleep with him to talk him into anything, EVER. But when she got her way, sometimes she gave him a little reward, and sometimes that reward included a finger up his ass. He was a cute old man, and she knew she was his little treasure. They played it down in the office, but she didn't have to fuck him to make him feel good. No, old men were more 'gentlemanly', and just being in the company of a fine woman made all the difference in the world. To an older man with distinguished tastes, the company of an elegant woman was a greater thrill than sex, and he was one of those gentlemen.

"ALL RIGHT! GO TO CANADA! BUT I WANT TWO THOUSAND WORDS, AND I WANT IT IN MY INBOX IN ONE WEEK!" She laughed and gave him a wink as he stormed out of the meeting room and back into his office where his secretary handed him coffee, a doughnut, and started rubbing his back. Brenda ran to the Teletype room, grabbed all of the printouts of her story, and head out to the one place all good investigative reporters know to get the background on their stories- the library.

CHAPTER FOUR

It has been called the Kaptar in the Russian Caucuses, Chuchuna in North East Siberia, Almas in Mongolia, Kangmi in Tibet, Sasquatch in Canada, and Bigfoot in the United States. The topography and exact map points of the locations were easy enough to pinpoint through GPS systems, but the internet couldn't reproduce the vast amount of information that old books in the library held on subjects studied before 1990, when the internet really started taking off. If you wanted to download and flip through a million pages on your laptop it was possible, but nothing could replace the feeling of gathering a dozen old books around you, making notes and placing stick it notes in the pages, and soaking up as much quality information as you could.

Brenda loved libraries. Not only did she consider them one of the greatest and best loved inventions of civilization, they were quiet, almost holy, like churches or synagogues, and people left them smarter than when they walked in. Not a lot of places can make that claim. Many libraries, like in Boston and London, also held great works of art along with priceless manuscripts written by kings, popes, saints, legends that would come to life as you directly entered their minds by reading the exact words they wrote so people would understand and the world would grow. There was something different books held that reporting just couldn't replace, and though they were both methods of transferring information, books were written BY the subject (for a large part) and reporting was written ABOUT the subject.

The other thing she loved about libraries was the little hidden stack in the lower levels and cubby holed computers in little cubicles way in the back. She had met, seduced, and fucked more cute boys in those little private areas of the library than probably anyone else, she guessed. She could tell there were a few 'nerd groupies', girls who had the hots for smart guys and hung around libraries and science fairs the way that Hollywood starlets hung around L.A. Kings hockey games, but these were amateurs compared to her, and every once in awhile she spotted a guy completely wrapped up in a book about physics or chemistry, and she couldn't help but walk over and find out what he was reading. She loved the way their eyes popped out of their head when she hiked up her skirt and straddled their thighs, rubbing her pussy against their not very trendy jeans. Guys like this almost never got hit on, and that's what made it so much fun for her. Macho guys in nightclubs showing off and expecting girls to swoon were such a bore, but guys like this were sure to worship her forever. That's why it was such an easy decision to run her hand up their legs and stroke their dicks in the library after just meeting them...It was a memory they would treasure forever, and she always wanted to be a guy's favorite wet dream girl.

Today she wasn't on that kind of a hunt. Today, she had to brush up on as much as she could about cryptozoology, or the study of undiscovered and unnamed animals. This included all kinds of sea monsters, myths and dragons, well known stories like the chupacabra and the mothman, and they were all lumped together in books that also included stories, maps, pictures, and descriptions of her latest prey, Bigfoot. Had someone told her even two weeks ago that she would soon be crawling through the Canadian wilderness looking for a sasquatch, she would have told them they were out of their minds. But here she was, getting ready to load an airplane up with her camera guy, some camping equipment, and whatever tools she thought she would need to get this hot little bitch she saw on the office computer to walk her through what happened when she disappeared.

The thing Brenda didn't forget was that the GIRL never mentioned any kind of beast; it was the search and rescue guys who found the prints. She believed her friend who called her enough that it was worth investigating, because there was nothing in it for him, no money, no fame, but I think maybe he had fond memories of her last visit there. She did a piece on the disappearing lands of the native Canadians, then joined him in his cabin for a night with a wild forest man, and to be honest, it was a fond memory for her as well.

As she scribbled notes and locations she found in her books, she also made a list of things to be packed. All of the usual necessities for an outdoors adventure would have to go, plus the little comforts of home, and then there were the personal touches- lubricant, mini vibrator, hot panties, lotion, and handcuffs. A girl just can't travel without her handcuffs. After she was satisfied with her research and her travel list, she packed it in at the library and went back to pick up Brian with all of his gear and her travel vouchers at the Tribune building. Brian was going to spend the night, and then first thing tomorrow they would be on a plane to the Canadian wilderness.

The last piece of the puzzle was getting the girl to confirm to an interview. She had been in a trance like state ever since being found, and though the police said that she had no injuries other than minor bruises on her thighs and arms, she was in remarkably good shape for someone who had been lost in the forest for a month. This was how they were sure someone had been taking care of her, keeping her warm, and feeding her. They also said that she had a smile on her face that wouldn't come off, almost as if she was in a little dreamland, and hadn't come back to reality yet. Well, we'd just have to see about that.

The family had agreed to let Brenda try and talk to her. They remembered her from the story she had done in that area years ago, and this was why she tried to help out where she could. There were dozens of other publications and websites begging for interviews, many of them offering substantial amounts of money, but the one thing you could always count on with country people was integrity. When Brenda's name came up, she was given first chance to try and talk to the girl, and in about twenty hours, she was going to try to find out if the girl had in fact been kidnapped by Bigfoot.

CHAPTER FIVE

Camera equipment loaded and the crew in check, (well it was just Brian but Brenda LOVED referring to him as "the crew", partially because it made it made her sound more professional, and partially because it made him sound like her underling and she KNEW he HATED that), she spent an hour or two getting herself prettied and perfumed to be the most appealing to what she assumed was (up to this point anyway) a straight woman. She had dozens of different looks for different seductions, and she loved slipping into them as often as possible. It made her feel like a superhero, and gave her an extra boost of confidence that couldn't be put into words. She had looks that she knew would entice Chinese businessmen, looks that appealed to Arabian princes, clothes that turned on U.S. senators, baseball players, rock stars, astronauts.

If she was going to meet an interview subject for the first time, the most valuable piece of information she could get on them was a picture of their significant other. From this she could deduce little clues that were invisible to the naked eye. From looking at the way a Turkish monarch's wife dressed, she could tell if he loved having his balls licked or if he wanted to suck on her toes. She could look at a Japanese businessman's wife and know if she had to pack her little schoolgirl outfit or black leather. She was as clever as they came, and she knew that people's perversions were the things they tried to hide the most. She looked for the things that were missing, and from this she could tell what they really wanted. If an older man was overly affectionate with his wife, he was trying to hide from the world the fact that he was a closet homosexual. ALL partners who have been together that long are at each other's throats too much to make a scene in public, unless they're in the company of their employer. It was things like this that gave her the sexual edge, and the ability to seduce and befriend the most powerful people in the world.

For this girl, she packed the basic necessities for an outdoor camping trip, to look boyish and woodsy. Flannel shirts, jeans, hiking boots, and Gore-Tex all found her way into her bag, but to get girls like this, girls who had very little or no experience with women, she knew what to pack. The best way to seduce a straight girl was to do what she called the 'Cinderella' transformation. She packed two slinky, sexy outfits for a night out at an expensive nightclub (paid for by the newspaper, of course)- one for her, and one for, "Oh, I'd love to take you out for a night to say thanks for meeting with me. We'll pay for the whole night, so get ready to have fun! What's that? You don't have a THING to wear? Hmm, well, I have this old thing I was going to wear to an awards show on a stopover on the way back, but here, try it on!" And then she would help her target into the sexiest designer dress she had ever put on, and spend a good half hour brushing her face with expensive powders and perfumes. By the time she was done, Brenda had done such a seductive and erotic dance for them, dressing them, complementing them on their body, that they practically JUMPED her before they even left the hotel, and if they did, that was fine with her. If there was any part of the story they left out before that, inadvertently or not, it spilled out as they lay on the pillows, dripping with sweat. Brenda loved her job.

They booked a private twin for the week, and knew the pilot well. He was on as many assignments as they could get him on, especially when crossing borders. There were only three languages you needed to know in the western hemisphere, French, English, and Spanish. All of the other ones, Hawaiian, German, different dialects of Aztec, always had someone who spoke one of the major languages close by. James, their pilot, spoke French, English, and Spanish fluently, and knew air traffic controllers and customs agents from the Arctic circle down to the Straits of Magellan. All he had to do was radio ahead that he was coming, and customs inspectors never asked them to land or met them at the airstrip. He was not just a convenience, he was a necessity, and he got paid well. He had been a combat pilot in Afghanistan, and knew how to crash better than anyone else. He had been shot down three times in three different aircraft, and there was never a fatality. He kept his cool in the most stressful situations, so what the hell was it to him if dope dealers were running after the camera crew, guns blazing? He'd simply grab an Israeli made UZI machine gun he kept under the seat, leaned out the window, and let fly, motor running, door open. The dopers would hit the floor, the camera crew flung their gear in the plane, and they got into the air as he unloaded his whole clip and got the plane in the air at the same time. He wasn't just a pilot, he was a fucking MAGICIAN, and Brenda had rewarded him more that a few times for saving her skin.

James knew the way to Quebec by heart, and the plane was soon in the air. As soon as they were airborne they had a little ritual that was meant to 'bless' the assignment, for they all knew that every assignment, whether to the deserts of Arabia, the jungles of the Amazon, or the mountains of Nepal, could be their last, so they threw a little party to celebrate their friendship and lives. Brenda broke out the Champagne and caviar, and James and Brian heated up some steak strips and brought out chilled shrimp cocktails. The airplane was on autopilot, and they all knew enough about aeronautics that they all felt comfortable with the airplane under computer control.

These days computers flew planes better than people did, so it was no problem to leave the controls. The computer could see clearer, better, and farther than a human could, it could respond to difficult weather anomalies faster. It could steer through mountain ravines and gullies with lightning speed, and it could do it all without any human intervention at all. The computer knew the difference between a cloud and a plateau, had the elevations of every radio tower in the world at instant access, and also had up to the second flight positions of every airborne craft in the world, so it was almost 99% safer leaving the computer in charge, and they all knew it.

Brenda had almost done a story about how the airlines used computers to fly over 99% of all commercial flights worldwide and how the pilot these days was just a nearly meaningless expense. What she found was that some airlines were lobbying to have pilots removed from the cockpits in order to reduce the cost of the flight by a drastic amount, and passing those savings on to allow more competitive ticket pricing, but she knew that customer confidence in toilet tissue and customer confidence in giant flying busses were two different things. She also found that human error was responsible for 100% of the air accidents that weren't mechanical failure, and computer error counted for zero percent of those same accidents. After months of digging, she found that people would rather have a human in the cockpit, whether he had anything to do with flying the plane or not, and have an increased chance of 9000% that there would be an accident, than to have an empty seat up front, and have almost NO chance of an accident. This was one of the rare stories she stepped away from. She didn't want to be responsible for consumer confidence in the airlines to drop to an all time low.

Knowing that the plane was in good hands, they proceeded to eat and drink all the way across the country. They told old battle stories, laughed about financial empires they had helped collapse, and people they wanted to try and get hold of again. They almost talked James into leaving the plane in the hangar and coming camping with them, because it seemed all he ever did was hang out at the airport, drink with the other pilots and do check ups on his airplane. For once, they wanted him to come on set with them, and this looked like the perfect adventure, but as usual he declined. He said he was happy waiting for them to come back with stories, footage, and all excited as they tried to get the onboard antennae to transmit their high definition footage to the nearest relay that would get it all to Los Angeles. This was tricky, because if it was intercepted, it could be blown by another Internet news source before they were able to get the whole story together, and news piracy was getting to be a bigger and bigger problem. Even with security codes and data scramblers, they were always thinking of new ways to outsmart hackers who would steal their footage directly from the airwaves, and transmit it over the net sometimes without the slightest clue of what they were transmitting. This could be extremely dangerous as well, because pictures transmitted without commentary could be misconstrued in a thousand different ways, and it could cause a lot of people very, very expensive problems.

They flew over the deserts of Nevada and Utah, smoking joints of very good herb and enjoying the scenery along with strawberries and Champagne. They flew over the endless expanse of corn and potato fields of the north, and Brenda was glad she didn't have to do this story in the winter, when it would have been ten below zero in the daytime, and they would have had to snuggle together in their tents at night. Well, she wasn't ENTIRELY missing that, but they could do that in their room at the Hilton. As they crossed over the border into Canada, they gave a little cheer and mapped out the rest of their course. It was only going to be another two hours before they landed in that remote airstrip in Quebec, and from there they would have one of the local newsmen from their affiliate news agency in Canada drive them to the hospital where they would see the girl. Since they left early in the morning, it was only a seven hour flight and they would get to her by five or six o'clock that evening. Brenda was hoping that after a good night of 'getting to know you' and general questions, she would be willing to talk about what happened to her.

They all looked out over the expanse of the great wilderness of Canada in awe of the sheer size and magnitude of the forests and lakes. It ALL seemed to be untouched by man. Flying over the United States, you knew that there had been civilizations there for a long time. For at least fifty miles in every direction surrounding every large city, there was urban sprawl, factories, markets, offices, parks and recreational facilities, utility centers like power stations and telephone centers, and housing. Any place that wasn't desert or lake was usually converted into farmland, and even the forests didn't go on for very long before an ocean of green or brown crops sat in an orderly fashion on the ground, signifying that this land had ALL been tamed, and it was all spoken for. Canada, however, was still her own master, and it would take HUNDREDS of years for any civilization to conquer her. She was majestic in her sheer scale, as thousands of square miles of untouched forests and mountains sat unused as ski resorts, unused as jet ski rental vacation spots, unused as logging and Christmas tree farming territory. Of course Canada had these things, but the distances in between the cities was almost total forest, and Brenda assumed largely uninhabited except by the occasional gold miner, solitary hunter, and the few indigenous Native tribes that occasionally dotted the landscape, preferring to live far away from the world of the white man, and having ample room to do so.

The farther away from civilization you got, the wilder and wilder the territory became. Entire herds of elk, reindeer, caribou, moose, and every kind of duck, geese, and waterfowl celebrated in abundance their ability to stretch out and fearlessly enjoy their open spaces. Brenda couldn't help thinking that the Canadians went out of their way to keep most of the scenic forests, waterfalls, lakes, and rivers out of camping brochures and wilderness magazines. As different as Canadians were from Americans in their habits and customs, she felt that there was an unspoken law that they wanted to preserve as much of this wilderness as possible, and the thought of any more of it being exploited to loggers, travel agents, ski hill investors, and real estate developers made them cringe.

Almost all Canadians had been to the United States as children as an excuse to visit museums and giant shopping malls and candy factories (or so their parents said), but in reality they wanted the children to know early on what Canada would turn into if they allowed every greedy American developer to turn every plot of land, every lakeside beach, every mountain slope, every frozen river, and every field of running elk into some kind of money making tourist attraction. They saw the horror not only in the fact that it would ruin the inherit beauty in all of these things, but the trails of candy bar wrappers, the cozy little fireplace taverns turned into Bud Lite promotional sights with bikini girl posters and swarms of college kids on spring break trashing the place, the water skiing assholes turning peaceful fishing sites into rolling, noisy party zones by inbred jocks on jet skis, and the beautiful green moss and mushroom covered forest floors turned into mushy black mud by campers wearing brand new Timberland boots their parents had ordered for them from L.L. Bean. Brenda knew that Canadians acted out of their minds for a reason, and rightfully so. The great thing about it was that it worked, and up until now, they had kept the Americans out except for a few mining claims, oil strikes which made them all rich, and National Geographic and similar magazines which catalogued the native wildlife and strengthened their causes even more.

People who wanted to get rich lived in the madhouse world of the inner cities of the United States, and to an outsider, especially one from a serene environment like the majestic forests of Canada, the U.S. cities were insane asylums filled with absolute batshit crazy lunatics. People in the U.S. couldn't understand that not everyone was as greedy and materialistic as they were, and people from quiet rural areas couldn't understand how people could live in the middle of so much noise and commotion.

People who lived this far north lived up here because they valued their solitude, peace, and quiet, and went out of their way to make Canada not seem like a worthwhile travel and vacation destination. They didn't seem to consciously do it, but she could never recall any conversation where a Canadian talked about how great their country was, as all other patriots do. No, this was something she felt that they wanted to keep to themselves, and looking out over the beautiful and majestic countryside, she couldn't blame them. As the plane slowed and descended into the grandeur of the Canadian forests, they all got ready to disembark looking like a professional news crew and not like a bunch of sex and drug-crazed degenerates. They had this part down cold, and James was first to get a once over from Brenda, making sure there was no coke falling out of his nose, and the smell of alcohol was hidden from his breath, then she gave his face a quick wash and his uniform a few brushes and sat him back into the pilot seat. This wasn't the first time the plane had flown almost the entire journey by itself, and probably wouldn't be the last.

Brian and Brenda did a quick once over on each other and cleaned up the cabin. They were pretty sure not to encounter any customs agents or border patrols at the airport, since it was in such a rural setting and they had special clearance, but all it took was one butt hurt reject Brenda had spurned the advances of, and the next thing you knew there were dogs sniffing all over the plane. As much as Brenda tried to make everyone happy, some guys wanted more than their share. Unfortunately, some of those same guys still had their jobs in high ranking positions and more than once one of her rejected would be lovers tried to frame her for drug smuggling or spying. James and Brian had been more than instrumental in handling these situations and were always on the lookout for potential pitfalls, so they made sure to take special care when approaching sensitive situations like entering palaces, embassies, or crossing international borders.

Satisfied they had everything eaten, smoked, sniffed, safely stashed, or up someone's butt, they came to a soft landing in a small airstrip about fifteen miles from the hospital they would start their investigation at. There didn't look to be any customs cars or official looking vehicles on the ground as they came in so no one was worried, but they did a double quick check of the airplane just in case. The Cessna twin engine plane revved to a perfect landing amongst pine trees five stories high, and slowed to a perfect stop on smooth blacktop that looked like it only got used twice a year when some wilderness magazine or Standard Oil was in town. They rolled the plane up to a hangar, and noticed a Nissan Pathfinder with a cowboy-looking guy standing next to it. He seemed like the only one around, but that meant nothing. Plenty of times they had landed when there was only one or even NO people around, only to have the plane shot with a hail of machine gun fire, a bomb go off on the runway, or a team of soldiers start chasing them while they slammed the plane back into high gear and took the fuck off. This guy wasn't that kind or any kind of trouble though. He moseyed up to the plane the way only cowboys can mosey, and a smile ran across Brenda's face as the cabin door opened and she was once again standing face to face with Stewart Black Sky.

CHAPTER SIX

Stewart grinned a mile wide grin as Brenda jumped off the plane and into his arms. She couldn't help thinking there was nothing like the feel of a real cowboy, and this one was all man. He was part Texas ranger, part Yukon Miner, and part Chehalis Indian, which were a Northern Canadian tribe. Stewart was able to trace his family from parts all over the country from the early 1800's, and they had come from Texas, New Orleans, San Francisco, and Native Canada, and he had stories passed on from relatives on all sides of his family that they kept in books that circulated on the internet to all of their other relatives and blood relations. It was so much easier to keep track of your kin these days on the internet, and those who had taken the little bit of effort to keep stories from great grandparents alive were greatly rewarded, and Stewart was one of those guys whose families had built, and I mean LITERALLY built, Canada and the United States. Maybe he tried to carry it on him a little too obviously, with the giant brass belt buckle, the cowboy hat, boots, and rolled up cigarettes, but when that man was in a crowd of women, you almost had to run around to stop them all from fainting. There was something about a rugged outdoorsman that every woman loved, and Stewart knew it. Brenda loved it too, and she couldn't help thinking he was playing it up a bit just for her but that was the majesty of a real cowboy…. they have the ability to make every woman in the room think exactly that same thing.

After introducing the rest of the crew, they drove James to the hotel and went straight to the hospital where Emily had been recovering. Stewart took the few minutes they had to try and prep Brenda on what her condition was and what to try to expect, but Brenda already knew this was going to be a psychological battle, not an inquisition. Something made that girl keep quiet about what had happened to her, and Brenda's guess was that she was terrified of what they would do to her if she told. She had a vast amount of experience with women like this, ones who had been rescued from their boyfriend pimps, or scumbag mafia sex traffickers, girls who were in fear for their lives. Brenda wasn't going to make her talk if she didn't want to; she was going to make her feel safe. If she was able to make her feel safe, and then she wanted to talk after that, well then that was okay.

They pulled up at the hospital and Brenda promised to connect with Stewart in a few days, but first she had to get her story. Stewart wasn't just a sexy cowboy; he was a smart and congenial man who understood when to leave a girl to her work. They said their goodbyes, but Brenda couldn't help noticing the bulge in Stewart's pants was about twice as big after they hugged. He gave that little cowboy smile and wink that only cowboys can do, and Brian grabbed the camera gear and followed Brenda into the hospital. As they walked the halls Brenda couldn't help noticing that there were three very sacred places on earth that were at the forefront of human endeavor and experience, and were the most debated and argued about in terms of quality and expense, yet were the most quiet places civilized man patronized; these were hospitals like she was in now, churches, and libraries. As she walked the halls of the hospital looking for Emily's room, she couldn't help noticing that people went out of their way to whisper to each other, the way they do in churches and in libraries, and decided to get herself into existential conversations like this one when she wasn't on assignment.

After taking the elevator up to the third floor, they came up to the nurses' desk to ask for Emily's room.

"Oh, they're expecting you. The family's in the room just there to the right, they would like to speak to you before you see their daughter".

That was fine with Brenda. She could calm or charm the pants off of anyone, and having to talk to the parents, guardian, doctor, teacher, jailer, or whomever was in charge of her interview subject was going to have their say, and she would nod her head and agree ONE HUNDRED PERCENT with whatever their wishes were, not to mention macaroni salad, not to cross your legs, not to ask 'why did you suck the eyeballs out of your victim's heads?' There was always a clown outside the door who had tried to do her job before her, and they always fucked it up in one way or another, and thought it their duty to inform her that the fucked up thing they did was not in fact THEIR fault, but an idiosyncrasy of the subject that would drive them into a rage if she repeated their mistake. Brenda knew how to placate these amateur interrogators, but when she got the subject alone, they were all hers.

"OH MY GOD! BRENDA NOVA! I AM SUCH A HUGE FAN OF YOURS!!" The women of Emily's family gushed all over her, shaking her hand and telling her how fabulous she looked. Brenda ALWAYS returned the complement, and the best way was to be sincere, so she worked with what she had. "Emily is YOUR daughter? She is such a GORGEOUS creature, I'm not surprised at all you ladies are related to her, what a BEAUTIFUL family!" To which they all gushed "Awwwww" and turned in a modest fashion. These rural Canadian women who were built for chopping holes in the lake for fishing in winter and sawing logs in the fall, and didn't normally haunt the makeup and fragrance counters at Macy's. Nor did they shop at Lord and Taylor's, so Brenda was always extra careful to bring a few silk scarves, a few (fake) fur lined gloves, and a few unopened trial bottles of 'Oil of Olay' and "L'Air du Temp' to give to the women not right away, but at the right time- too early and they seemed like bribes. If they were given later on they felt like gifts.

After the usual small talk, Brenda sat with Emily's mother to give her the proper respect before throwing all the advice she was about to give Brenda straight out the window, but it was a formality.

"Now Brenda, Emily has seen you on television for many years and is excited to meet you, but she still hasn't said a word. We're not sure what those barbarians did to her, but we're sure the guy she left to camp with didn't have anything to do with it. He's someone everyone in the town has known since he was born, and he was the first to come screaming into town and the first in the search party when she went missing, so he's not a suspect. We're not sure exactly who took care of her. So far she has refused to be examined for any signs of (and at this point she whispered "pre-marital infidelity"), nor has she mentioned how she was treated. Oh, I fear the WORST was done to that poor child! Locked up in a cabin or a cave by God knows WHAT kind of unholy men for their selfish, evil, sinful purposes, yet returned home with barely a scratch on her, thank the Lord!" (Brenda's thoughts were starting to wander, to be tied up, treated right, and used as a sex slave by a bunch of mountain men as sexy as Stewart Black Sky, now THAT was a kidnapping SHE wouldn't want to come home from either—"WAIT" Brenda interrupted the wailing and sobbing of the country women. "Didn't my report say that she initially didn't WANT to be brought home? Didn't she FIGHT her rescuers, even AFTER they identified themselves as Canadian Mounties?"

"Well yes, but at that point she had been in the wilderness for almost a month and ANYONE trying to grab her would have been suspect, no matter WHO they said they were. I mean, what if the first guys who grabbed her said they were from the forestry service and she needed to come with them, only to be tied up and abused in a cave or a cabin somewhere, and the next guy comes along saying the same thing, wouldn't you fight them as well?" Brenda though about that for a minute, and both theories made sense. She was either too afraid to leave because the new kidnappers could be worse than the old ones, or because the first ones threatened her and her family with death if she escaped and told, or even just escaped, and then there was the Stockholm Syndrome, where the victims identify with their kidnappers and don't want to leave because they've been brainwashed, but there was another possibility. Maybe Emily was taken to a place where she was treated like a queen and had a lover she always wanted to look out for her. Maybe, just maybe, this lover was what she had been looking for in a man from day one, and having found him, was reticent to let go.

With Emily's family looking over their shoulders, Brian and Brenda slipped as quietly into her room as possible. Brian tried to be as unobtrusive about setting up camera equipment as he could, not an easy thing to do, but when you've got Brenda leaning over you, a sexy, voluptuous, olive skinned, hourglass shaped vixen pouring Champaign and dishing out cheese stuffed Portobello mushrooms, it's easy to ignore a guy setting up and wiring an entire Canon fx-h1 high def video capture system and a few Neumann condenser microphones running into a Mackie powered digital console, all prewired and configured for any occasion by our own audio/video tech guru. He could have a dozen clip on mics for a line of Israeli soldiers as fast as he could drop a boom microphone into a tomb in the process of being grave robbed and get it ALL on tape, because the ONE thing he did BEFORE setting up a massive multichannel system was to set up an inexpensive (but HIGHLY sensitive) STEREO microphone that would STILL pick up every word said, you just wouldn't have it on twenty four discrete channels, you'd have it on two channels, but that's where Brian's artistry came in. IF there was a statement that was caught in tape but was too jumbled with background noise to get a clear picture of what was said, Brian had a library of THOUSANDS of search algorithms that would interpolate the voice structures, cut out the noises that did NOT belong to the target, and isolate the voice you DID want. So out of a crowded room, if you plopped a stereo microphone at the top and had a sample of the target voice you were trying to isolate, you could enter the frequency, timbre, oscillation of the voice you were trying to either isolate or eliminate, and within a few hours and after about three gallons of jolt cola, red bull, or whatever liquid speed was available to you at the time, a full bottle of Visine, and a few Adderall to keep your spirits up, by morning Brian could have you an audio tape of the British surrendering to George Washington if that's what you wanted.

With the cameras hooked up, microphones in place, and Emily's family safely out of range, Brenda sat on the hospital bed and held Emily's hand. For the first time she was really able to look at her up close, and they seemed to be lost in each other's eyes as if to say, "Is this really you? Are you really here?" Emily took in Brenda's sophisticated clothing, elegant fragrances, and worldly charm, and Brenda was in awe of Emily's natural beauty, deep, deep blue eyes, and the fact that she had just lived through an experience that someone would probably make a movie out of in the near future, but both of them were hoping that they would be friends. Emily, quiet as a church mouse, let out a little "are they gone yet?" to which Brenda smiled and nodded yes. They were all outside and there was someone to watch the door to make sure no one came in.

"Oh good, they've been pestering me for the last few days about movie rights, book deals, even offers from third rate magazines for an exclusive story, and every one in my family wants to be the first to get a piece of the action, so I've had to play it dumb since I was brought in. I had no idea my family was so greedy. I was sure they were going to protect me from all of these scumbag newsmen, but my own family members have turned out to be more greedy than the reporters they're supposed to be keeping me safe from!" Brenda had seen plenty of girls like this, and they all wanted reassurance that they weren't going to get fucked for their story, or make some scumbag, even if it was a member of their own family, rich. Sharks were swimming all around people in these situations, and Emily had done the smartest thing that anyone could possibly do, and that was to keep her mouth shut.

"Don't worry, honey, you're in good hands. Emily, you know as well as I do that someone was out there with you taking care of you, and everyone wants to know who it was, what happened, and why you were released, or if you in fact escaped, and how you did it. All I'm here for is to help you tell your story, and until you do, you're going to be pestered until the day you die. SO it's my job to get us to work together on this. All I need is a satisfactory story, and that will take care of whatever secrets you want to keep, and I have a feeling that there are a lot of things you don't want anyone else to know. That's fine dear, and if I were in your shoes, I probably wouldn't want the whole world knowing my business either, but we HAVE to tell them something, and that something has to be believable. Are we on the same page so far?"

Emily slowly nodded her head yes, more like a kid who was caught being naughty at school than a girl who was hiding one of the scientific marvels of the twenty first century in her memory. Emily recognized this type of behavior, and knew the right path to take.

"First thing we're going to do is go out for a nice dinner and a few drinks, complements of the Los Angeles Media Center, how does that sound?" Emily IMMEDIATELY brightened up, and nodded her head enthusiastically, as if she were being paroled from this prison of relatives and lawyers trying to get her to sign papers and exclusive rights to her story she didn't want to sign. "That'll get us all relaxed and help you forget about the past few weeks. I figured you could use a break from all of this. Tell you what. I know a nice little nightclub with a restaurant about an hour south of here in Umiujaq, right on the bay that's far enough away from here that there'll be no crowds, no family, and we can get shitfaced drunk and no one will know who we are except for a couple of drunk college co-eds, and we'll have two bodyguards to make sure nothing happens to us. Sound like fun? "

Emily was grinning from ear to ear as she said "YYYYEEEAAAAA!!!" to each one of Brenda's suggestions. "There's one thing though. The story has been on the news all over the country. How can we go anywhere without being recognized?" Brenda looked over at Brian, who was outside handing out trinkets and high end trial size bottles of brand name goop to Emily's family and said, "Honey, things like that are my specialty. By the time I get done with you, no one, not even your own family, will know who you are."

Brenda flipped open her magic suitcase full of expensive evening wear and started hanging things all over the room, then opened the door and started shouting to the crowd outside, "EXCUSE ME, WE'RE GOING TO NEED SOME- sir, that is NOT a shaving cream- PRIVACY FOR A FEW. CAN WE HAVE THE FAMILY WAIT IN THE CHAPEL DOWN THE HALL PLEASE? AND BY ALL MEANS CONTINUE TO–miss, that is NOT for rubbing on your feet, nor is it.... oh, never mind- PRAY FOR EMILY'S RECOVERY. WE WILL NEED COMPLETE SILENCE WHILE QUESTIONING HER, SO PLEASE GIVE US AS MUCH ROOM

AS POSSIBLE". Emily's family had been making so much noise over the trial size bottles of Caesar's Palace shampoo and Oil of Olay samples they gooped on each other, expecting instant results, that they realized the noise they were making and moved on down the hall to perform their newfound witchcraft elsewhere.

Finally alone, Brenda began gently unfolding silk slips, satin bras, and French cut panties she knew that Emily probably didn't have in her closet.

"Let's start with a bath, shall we?", to which Emily blushed.

"It's time you treated yourself to a little 'me' time. That's what we call it in the city. " Brenda turned the water on very warm and let it fill the tub with giant bubbles she NEVER forget to bring with her. While the tub was filling, Brenda stood Emily up from her hospital bed, and walked over to the door to make sure it was locked. She knew that Brian was standing guard outside. It was part of his job, after all. With the door locked and the lights low, Brenda slowly unzipped her expensive business dress so that it slipped off over her hips with a 'swish' that made it essential for her to wiggle her hips in a very seductive fashion to ensure the skirt fell to the floor, leaving her in a sheer, soft, silky slip. Emily couldn't take her eyes off of Brenda as she sauntered towards her, both of their breathing getting heavier and heavier, as if they were both hypnotized and powerless over what was to come next. They both wanted it to happen, and Brenda could tell Emily was a little bit scared, but that gave her an extra thrill.

Brenda walked into the bathroom and felt the water, which was full enough so that the bubbles were flowing over the sides and making little mountainscapes in the tub, perfect for the modesty of a young girl. She grabbed Emily by the hand, and leading her over to the tub, turned her around and slowly untied the straps on the back of her gown. When she finished the last one, Emily held the gown up with her hand as if it was her last bastion of false modesty, but even Brenda knew she couldn't help wanting to show off those c-cup breasts that drove all the Canadian boys on campus crazy with desire. "Don't worry honey, I won't look". Brenda casually said, though they both wanted it to be a lie, she still said it so Emily could retain her ladylike image. Brenda slipped the gown over her shoulders, revealing a perfect hourglass shape, beautiful shoulders that curved like a violin down to her waist, and curving again at her heart shaped ass. This one Brenda couldn't resist. She ran her fingernails down along the small of Emily's back, over the round tops of her waist, and below where her ass cheeks met the tops of her legs. Emily let out a slight gasp as Brenda's fingertips felt the warmth of the space between her thighs, closer and closer to the spot where they met at the top of her legs, and they both felt the wetness that was beginning to betray both of their thoughts as they stood there, motionless, enjoying being pressed together, Emily's back into Brenda's breasts and hips, and Brenda's fingers now finding their way inside Emily's pussy, which was now dripping and making Brenda's fingers slide in with ease.

Brenda gave a slight shove towards the tub, and Emily complied, stepping into the warm sudsy water and sitting into what felt like heaven. Brenda slowly removed the rest of her clothes while Emily watched, first sliding her satiny beige colored dress blouse off one button at a time, and then undoing her silk bra that held her firm and gorgeous breasts up for the world to admire. Emily couldn't take her eyes off of them, and was in complete awe of the fact that this television superstar wanted to share a bath with her, much less interview her. Emily decided that she would try to make it a bath that Brenda would remember for a long, long time. Listening for any signs of noise outside and sure that they were alone, Brenda slipped into the tub with Emily running her hands up Brenda's long, smooth, tan colored legs. Even the space between her legs was shaven, and only the top of her pubic mound had any inclination that she had any hair at all down there. Emily had seen PLENTY of naked women before, and even seen plenty of naked girls on the pornos that the lumberjacks brought back from the cities, but those girls were shaved bald, and the local women weren't shaved at ALL, in fact it hadn't looked like they had been trimmed in their whole LIVES. It was a jungle down there, and not attractive at all. Her own grooming was minimal, but she felt a thrill run up her spine as Brenda Slipped in between her legs, came close to her face and kissed her gently on the lips. Sliding back a bit, she produced a Gillette triple blade razor and proceeded to raise Emily's hips up on to her knees. Emily's pussy was now more exposed to anyone than it ever had been, and she was excited beyond belief. She wasn't ashamed, or afraid, she was excited to be in control of this famous city woman, this woman who wanted to be her lover for the night, and this was a great place to start.

Brenda scooped up a handful of soap and water, spread it all over Emily's spread open pussy and rubbed gently, and Emily moved her hips along with the motion. It felt good.....sooooo goooood, it was just fucking hypnotic to have this girl rub her slowly back and forth, wetting and soaping her hand at just the right times. She felt herself getting wetter and wetter by the second, inside and out. Every once in awhile, Brenda brought the razor across the folds of her pussy, starting on the skin of the outside, soooo gently rubbing it upwards and taking a patch of hair with it, then scooping up a handful of water and dousing it to clean it so that it was smooth as a baby's butt. Emily couldn't help watching what Brenda was doing, and the more she watched, the wetter she became, wanting Brenda to rub her hand more and more all over her pussy. When both sides were finished, and Brenda was gently rubbing Emily's semi bald pussy where it had once been a hairy scene, she gingerly grabbed Brenda's finger and inserted it inside of her, leaning back and moaning, begging to be brought to a climax. Brenda took the cue and raised Emily's hips up on her thighs so that her knees were under Emily's back and Emily's freshly shaved pussy was up in the air on top of Brenda's thighs up to her stomach, Brenda leaned down and put her tongue inside Emily's mouth, and they explored each other and kissed the soft, gentle kiss only two women can do, dying for more. Brenda scooted Emily up so that her head was on top of the bathtub railing, and her freshly shaved pussy was still up in the air on Brenda's knees, and Brenda knelt down and parted Emily's pussy with her fingers and started to lick the outside of her vulva, teasing and kissing as if it were a sweet fruit that had to be licked for taste before it was eaten, and with Emily moaning "OOOOOHHHhhhhhh......uuuuunnnnnnhhhhhh..........hhhh hhhhhh.........hhhhhhhhhhhh.........." as if she was about to run out of air, Brenda licked the outside of Emily's pussy, all of the areas that had just been shaved, knowing that was a sincere mind fuck, and also knowing that if felt INCREDIBLE. Emily splashed about, bucking her hips wilder and wilder, wanting more than anything to get fucked like a horse in heat, by a tongue or a finger or a cock or a dildo or ANYTHING JUST FUCK ME, and Brenda knew this kind of motion the girls was having, and at just the right time, THRUST her tongue into Emily's waiting pussy, jamming it all the way inside her so that her face was practically inside her pussy, wildly thrashing about, sucking her clit and fingering her ass, slowly at first but then getting a little soapy water on it and then shoving her lubricated finger all the way inside of Emily's tight ass, licking the inside of her pussy and sucking in her clit the way only a woman could. Emily was SO worked up by this foreplay she screamed "FUCK YEAH!! OOOH, FUCK ME! FUUUUCK ME!!!!! OH GOD! OH GOD! OOOOOHHHH GOODDDDDDD!!!!!!" And bucked her hips so wildly that water splashed all over the floor and she squeezed Brenda's head so hard with her thighs that Brenda's earrings cut little patterns into the side of her head.

Emily let out squeak and fell to the bottom of the tub exhausted, and finally noticed that Brenda's face was covered with the juice from her pussy, and let out a laugh and kneeled up and licked Brenda's face all over to get it all off. Neither of them minded, pussy juice tasted great and they both loved sharing it with each other. They licked it off of Brenda's face, then they rubbed each other's tongues together to get every delicious drop, then Brenda dove down to Emily's pussy to get some more, and they spent the next half hour draining each other of all of the delicious treat they could get. They bent each other over in the tub, licking each other from behind, fingering each other and shoving their soaked fingers in

66

each other's mouths, wetting their bent over asses and smacking their wet flesh with that sound that was the sound of unrivaled pleasure, licking, sucking, and rubbing each other clean. They got so clean that they had to have another shower after they were finished just to get clean after that.

"Now, what did you come here for again?" Emily asked, and they both fell on the bed, naked as the day they were born, and laughing and giggling like teenage girls at a pajama party which this reminded both of them of, and both had missed frightfully. Brenda loved her job.

CHAPTER SEVEN

"Okay gorgeous, now that I have your attention..." Emily laughed at Brenda's little joke. She had never fucked a celebrity before, even though every band that came through made sure someone was out in the crowd looking for hot girls to bring backstage, and she was always asked, but never accepted. "Oh, you mean that wasn't the interview?" Brenda laughed at Emily's joke just as hard, and they fell on the bed giggling like teenage schoolgirls. Brenda wanted to take Emily out to a nice dinner, mostly because she wanted to see that body zipped into the tight eveningwear that Brenda brought special for her to wear, but they would get to that later.

Brian was excellent at keeping everyone out of the room until Brenda gave a special signal they had worked out years ago, and every case was the news story of the decade to anyone close by (at least to the family and friends who were skulking around the action trying to get their name in print). Brenda finished getting dressed and put Emily back into her nightgown, slipping her back into her hospital bed with a quick kiss and a wink. After giving Brian the all clear, he let the family know that they could stop in the room to check on her.

Up to this point, not a single word had been spoken about Emily's disappearance, but that's the way Brenda worked. First, gain their trust, then, if circumstances prevailed, fuck their brains out, and THEN she would get the juiciest, most compelling confession, the human interest story of a lifetime. It didn't always happen in that order, but one way or another, Brenda could turn a kid getting caught shoplifting a gerbil at a Wal-Mart into the crime of the century. She just had an amazing way with words and with people so that she could get the best out of them, and she was able to communicate it all in a way that made it something everyone wanted to read and learn from.

This was why she fought Mel so hard for stories like this. Sure, the Japanese/ Chinese/ Taiwan summit would have been something to go down in history, but how many people would be DYING to read it? How could she make that story JUMP off of the pages so that everyone would be talking about it? The truth was, she couldn't. THIS story, from the first tag line she read off of the Teletype computer, THIS story was one EVERYONE was going to want to read and see pictures and video from, even though she didn't have FACT ONE about what had happened. THAT was what made it so compelling. She knew that everyone else in the world would be DYING to find out what happened to that girl and how she stayed alive in the wild, and she made sure to leak cut little bits of information and email a few pictures to friends at other media outlets. If they printed made up stories about marital relations between teenage coeds and Neanderthal Bigfoots and splashed Emily's picture all over the front pages of every scandalous tabloid and conspiracy website in the world, was that her fault? Brenda could always count on them for priming her story to be bigger than it would ever have been without their speculative imaginary conclusions and litigation provoking sensationalism. They were a necessary and colorful part of the game, plus they threw the wildest parties, especially when a lawsuit was dropped.

If it turned out that the girl had just found an abandoned ski cottage with some macaroni and cheese in it and was able to keep herself alive for a month, people would STILL want to read it after all of the buildup that had been given to it. This was the art form to the news industry and Brenda's gift for competitive journalism. It wasn't just great writing or a great story, it was the buildup, the rumors, the pictures, the secrets, making the UNKNOWN facts just as important and thought provoking, and when the right time came and the hammer fell on just the right front pages and nighttime news stations along with the internet up to the minute press releases, it wouldn't just be a story, it would be a benchmark in time for all people of the world to measure their lives by. Have you ever noticed that period movies that are based in a specific year in the past never fail to mention an event that everyone of that age could recall? The reason is that news events are much greater benchmarks of time than calendars are. If you mention a date, a year twenty five years past and asked people where they were and what they were doing, they might not be able to give you a very specific answer, but if you mention a news event, the death of a celebrity, a sports team winning a memorable world championship, a terrorist attack, it is much more easy for people to place themselves at the point where they were when that event happened, as most other people can remember the same event and it ties everyone together by a great universal clock that is a psychic longitude for measuring our lives. Where were you when JFK died? Where were you when the Challenger exploded? Where were you when the twin towers fell? I remember because it happened right around the time that girl was rescued from the woods, you remember, everyone thought she was captured by Bigfoot? If a story made it to that level, it couldn't possibly be any bigger, and she had taken this little fish of a story and turned it into a whale. This whale she was going to harpoon, drag into the bay, and give everyone a slice with her name and have the ambergris made into her signature fragrance. This fragrance had the slight musky, steak and flesh scented fragrance of Emily's hot pussy all over it, and Brenda was going to make her the most wanted and adored girl in the North American territories. Brenda couldn't help thinking once again, "I love my job."

Brenda gave Emily a quick wink and said, "We'll get to the interview after your family goes home for the night, but make sure they do, so then I can have you all to myself." Emily blushed at having this famous reporter, this icon of feminine power interested in her at all, much less wanting her alone for the whole night. Emily was the kind of girl who would shy away from other girls who had tried to kiss her in the past, but she wanted Brenda back in the tub, her wet body slipping and sliding all over her hands and her tits and her ass, and her fingers exploring every little hole she had. She had been properly seduced and wanted more. She nodded to Brenda as the door opened and Emily's parents came in the room with a hail of "My BABY!"'s, cleaned, combed, made up and pressed expecting the cameras to be on when they walked in. Brenda almost burst out laughing when Emily's parents looked around and there wasn't a camera in sight. They had obviously spent the last hour making themselves as presentable as possible for their adoring public, or at least for their neighbors who were sure to tune in.

They looked around the room, not sure what to say. Emily and Brenda couldn't contain themselves anymore, and burst into laughter. Emily's parents looked at each other as if they had just stepped in dogshit, and waited for the other to save them from whatever faux pas they made that was obvious to everyone except for them. Brenda decided to be a lady and let them off the hook.

"I've got everything I need for a preliminary report, Emily, but I'll have to come back in an hour or two to get your on camera interview, will that be alright?" Emily giggled and nodded, as her parents looked at her totally confused as to what they should do. They figured they should just be thrilled that their baby was back in one piece, cameras or not, and hugged and cried over her, thrilled that she was smiling and talking and seemed to be coming back to normal.

"Now It's going to take a few hours with the makeup and hair and everything, so if it's alright can I get a few words from the two of you in the morning?" motioning towards Emily's parents who nodded yes, instantly relieved that they hadn't missed their chance at their fifteen minutes of fame. "But I'm going to need Emily's complete concentration, so will it be alright if I come back in two hours and I'll sit with her for the rest of the night, then the two of you can come back in the morning? I promise not to leave her side until at least one of you arrives in the a.m., sound like a plan?"

Emily's parents nodded yes, and Brenda scooped up Brian and head towards the door with the appropriate thank you's and goodbye's and the 'can't WAIT to fuck

YOU again' look she gave to Emily, who gave it right back to her, only Emily's was MUCH more obvious. Only Emily's father caught it, but he could tell that was how EVERYONE looked at Brenda Nova. Even HE couldn't help watching the swish of her hips as she practically shut the hospital room door with them. Neither Brian nor Brenda said a word as they got in the cab and head towards the hotel. Brian knew damned well what had happened in that room, and was hoping, no, PRAYING, that Emily had only gotten Brenda warmed up, because just thinking of the two of them playing in the tub gave him a hard on he couldn't even TRY to hide. In fact, he just let it bump into car doors, let out little "OOFF!" sounds when a piece of equipment dropped on his lap, and carried his computer six inches in front of him as they walked up to their room.

He really didn't have to worry, because Emily was just an appetizer and the second Brenda opened her hotel room door, she yanked Brian in, fell to her knees, and unzipped his pants as fast as she could and stuffed his rock hard dick as far as she could into her mouth. She wasn't even playing around, and Brian could tell that Emily had just gotten her all worked up without a bit of satisfaction, which he was more than happy to provide. This was all premeditated, because all Brian could think about right now was pulling Brenda's hair back out of the way so he could watch her take his cock all the way to the back of her throat, jamming it in and out of her mouth sucking as hard as she could, wanting every inch of her body to get fucked, fucked as hard as she could get fucked, and her mouth was just a toy for Brian to jam as hard as he pleased to get started.... She wanted so much for him to shoot a load of hot white come all over her face, down her throat, all over her tits, she was just DYING for cock right now, and if Stewart or James the pilot were in the same hotel, they'd be getting assaulted so she could stuff her mouth with as much dick as she could, then she just wanted to get fucked from every angle, every position, until she came so hard that she ripped the bed sheets in half and screamed loud enough to bring the security guards.....

Brian was already up to speed, and pulled her mouth off of his dick with a single motion that had her bent over the bed and her skirt pulled up around her waist. He stuffed his face into her crotch, feeling the heat from her pussy and the wetness dripping through the lacy fabric. He bit her panties right below her ass and yanked hard with both hands, ripping the fabric in half, then pulled up hard so her swollen pussy lips were pulsing through the tear and dove in with his mouth, sucking in the delicious juice and driving his tongue up as far inside her as he could. He loved hearing her moan with pleasure as he grabbed her hips from behind and lifted them up so his mouth fit completely over her sex, and worked his tongue from her clit to the base of her hole, up inside her ass, and back down again. He was strong enough to completely control her and pick her up and down with his tongue far out, basically holding his face still and lifting her up and down, licking and sucking on her from behind while pumping her like she was a machine at the gym, and she loved every second of it. She couldn't take it any more.

"Just fuck me, Brian, come on, fuck me hard!" He loved hearing her beg for his dick, it made him feel like it was not only his obligation, but also his duty as a man to fuck the living daylights out of this woman. He loved thinking of all the men in the world watching her all over the world while she gave some news report, her dressing room assistant always making sure her tits stood straight up and gave them a little extra attention by licking and sucking on them right before she went on the air. It gave them that little bit of extra lift and blush to her cheeks that seemed like too much makeup, but Brian had caught Brenda and her vanity room servant in an assortment of compromising positions to know that glow wasn't makeup. It was one of the secrets of the trade, and a secret he kept well.

"Beg me for it. Tell me how bad you want it". He wanted her to beg him sweetly. He wanted to know that right now, he was the man that every other man in the world wanted to be, doing what every man in the world wishes they could be doing, but she wasn't in that kind of mood.

"GOD DAMNIT, PUT YOUR FUCKING COCK IN ME AND FUCK ME HARD RIGHT NOW OR I'LL OPEN THE DOOR AND GRAB THE FIRST GUY WALKING DOWN THE HALL!"

He knew she was serious and wasn't about to play subservient bad little girl. The spit that was flying out of her mouth as she screamed at him convinced him that she was out of her mind with pent up lust, between getting teased in the tub with Emily and getting licked like a melting summertime fudgesicle, she was about to explode and wanted his dick in her NOW. In that second, she went from being submissive to dominating Brian, and SHE grabbed HIM by the back of the head, lay down on the bed with her legs spread open and her lacy panties still ripped in half pulling up both sides of her pussy, but open in the middle where Brian had violently sliced them open with his teeth (and drove her insane doing it!). She ripped his belt and work jeans off along with his boxers in one swift motion, pulling the final waistband of his underwear over his rock hard dick with her toe like a seasoned professional and loved when his dick bounced like a diving board after being released from its flannel prison, and with one hand on his ass and the other guiding his dick into her dripping pussy she shoved her hips and gave his ass an extra dig with her fingernails to make sure the first thrust was extra hard, with an "UUUUHHHNNNN!!!" they slammed together in a wet mess of muscle, sex, flesh, sweat, and pleasure.

Brian drove his dick into her as hard and as fast as he could, pumping her pussy over and over again, pulling her hair out of her face so he could watch her bite her lips and feel her hair getting yanked just the way she loved it..."OH SHIT BRIAN IM GONNA COME DON'T STOP FUCKING ME OH GOD FUCK ME HARDER!!" Brian and Brenda knew each other pretty well by now, and Brian knew it was his turn to deliver. He picked up her ass while still on top of her and SLAMMED his cock into her while picking her up with cadence and rhythm, her hips slapping against his thighs "SMACK! SMACK! SMACK!" as he tore her shirt open and sucked her swollen tits, bouncing up and down with the action. He held her hands above her head so she was helpless, completely immobilized by him and squeezed her breasts with the other, guiding them into his mouth and biting on the nipples and playfully sucking them so they were swollen and red, the nipples pushing straight up to the sky as she felt the five o'clock shadow of his whiskers on her breasts, his face deep in her chest and she squeezed her elbows together to make her tits stand straight up for him.

She started screaming "DON'T STOP FUCKING ME OHHHH GOD DON'T FUCKING STOP!!!!!", and he pulled HARD on her hair, pulling her head back and biting her nipples as she started to go over the edge, then stuck three fingers in her mouth, which she closed her lips over and ran her tongue on them and sucked HARD, getting them all wet as he pulled her mouth open, stuck his own tongue inside of her mouth and pulled his wet fingers out....They licked each other's mouths as she started to climax, screaming, "YES!! OH, GOD, YES!! FUCK ME!! FUCK ME! " and he reached down and stuck two fingers DEEP in her ass while she screamed "OOOOOHHHH!!!!!!! FUCK YEAHHHH!!!!!!! FUCK ME! FUCK ME! FUUCKK MEEEE!!!!! And thrust up and down on the bed so her pussy, her ass and her mouth were all getting fucked, and Brian, loving having her like this, couldn't hold it any longer. She could feel his cock swell with his come ready to shoot inside of her, and she grabbed both sides of his ass with her fingernails and DUG into his flesh, making him pump her even HARDER, and with both of them screaming "OOOOHHH FUUUUCK!!!" Brian shot his white hot load so deep inside of her that it lubricated her pussy even more and Brenda kept coming and coming screaming "FUCK YEA! SHOOT INSIDE MY FUCKING PUSSY FUCK ME HARDER DON'T STOP OH GOD!!!" Brian kept shooting more and more come inside of her, then THRUST as hard as he could, driving his dick home one final time and slapping their skin together so hard they had little rug burns on their thighs, and Brian moved his fingers around in her ass and her eyes popped open and they froze for a second, savoring the moment and making it last as long as they could, then finally collapsing on the bed in a heap of sweat, limbs, come, saliva, skin, hair, and ripped up clothes.

Brian pulled his fingers out of her ass SLOWLY, wrapping his fingers in a towel and laying beside her, still moving his dick in and out of her while she bucked her hips in motion, wondering if they should go for it again right now or wait until they rested for a few. They were both so happy at that moment they had completely forgotten why they were here, and for that matter, it took Brian a few seconds to remember what town or even country they were in. He smiled at her and she smiled back, neither saying a word. They didn't have to. That was the beauty of their relationship and why so many others fail. There were no words that could make that moment any better, so why spoil it? They collapsed next to each other exhausted, and Brian ran his hands over her breasts, which they both loved. They both had the same thought;

"I can't BELIEVE I'm getting paid for this."

CHAPTER EIGHT

After meeting up with James for dinner, they got their game plan together for the interview later this evening. All they had to do was to get Emily alone, and Brenda would do the rest. The hard part was going to be getting rid of the family, and they were hoping they wouldn't be the types to hang around trying to get in the shots or be interviewed, and both Brenda and Brian were hoping that Emily was taking care of that. Brenda would get a few seconds of them on tape, but it had to be tomorrow morning. If you asked the relatives a few questions before the big interview, the tended to hang around to see if they could be of any more help, or sometimes they just liked hanging around to watch what was going on, either way it just got too crowded and the subject never gave a completely candid interview with their wives or parents or kids around.

They telephoned ahead to see if Emily was still up for being on camera tonight, and Brenda assured her that she was bringing makeup and a dress so that she wouldn't look like a girl who just crawled out of the Canadian wilderness surviving on berries for a month. In exchange, Emily would get rid of the rest of her family, whom she assured Brenda didn't want to be on television, they were just happy and excited to have their baby back safely. They all breathed a sigh of relief, and were excited about meeting up for the evening. Brenda had everything she needed for just this type of assignment. She packed makeup (which she was a PRO with- you wouldn't BELIEVE the Afghani cave women Brenda was able to make look like "Beverly Hills Housewives" after an hour of personal touches and convincing them that their burkas were considered enslavement by the rest of the world), clothes to make Emily look seductive for the rest of the world (another specialty of hers), and a few relaxing pharmaceuticals to take the edge off if she got nervous when the camera was rolling. Brian was also a pro at making people relax in front of the lens, and he was a terrific flirt with women when they were nervous, making them laugh and telling them the camera wasn't on when he was actually getting his best stuff. Brenda watched him dress in tight black jeans and a dark new V-neck sweater, soft and fuzzy, in which he was a girl's wet dream.

With the camera packed in the rental car and Brenda and Brian smelling sweet and looking sharp, they left for the hospital. On their way up to the room they ran into Emily's parents who were thankfully on their way out, but left a number with Brenda in case Emily needed anything. Brenda could be very reassuring in these cases, and seemed to almost have a Florence Nightingale effect on people who were injured or traumatized. Brian had seen her hold a dying man who had been shot in the sternum and get the most beautiful, poetic diatribe from him on film as his last breaths left his lungs. It was if she was a sister of mercy with a camera over her shoulder, and it was one of her many gifts that made her one of the top investigative reporters in the world.

Brian sat outside for a few minutes, and Brenda sashayed into Emily's room, smiling at her and noticing that Emily was freshly showered and dressed in new hospital whites. Brenda leaned over and gave her a kiss after looking to make sure the door was closed, but then made sure it was a long, sensual, lover's kiss, and Emily smiled and blushed. Brenda could tell she had never been with a woman before, and loved seducing her little 'virgins', as she called them. "Okay honey, now that I have you all to myself, I am going to make you a STAR!" and with that, Brenda unzipped the travel bag she had with her and pulled out a light beige cashmere sweater that buttoned fashionably up the side and plunged dangerously in the neckline, something she knew would enhance the size of Emily's gorgeous breasts. She also pulled out a black half skirt, slit up the side in a not too modest fashion, along with nude colored nylons and four-inch heels. Any higher and Emily would look like she was trying too hard to be sexy, and Brenda knew right where to draw the line.

"But FIRST, I get to apply a little 'movie magic'. " Brenda opened her makeup case, which looked more like a fisherman's tackle box, with layers and layers of different colored pens, brushes, eye shadows, lipsticks, everything you needed to look like a star. Emily clapped her hands and squealed with delight as Brenda sat her up in the chair, pulled up another one so she was face to face with her, and looked her deep in the eyes. Emily blushed and looked down, embarrassed at the attention from such an exotic and glamorous star, but Brenda lifted her face up by placing one finger under her chin, then kissed her tenderly on the lips, saying, "Are you ready?" Emily nodded yes, and they got to work.

Brian quietly lurked in the dark shadows of the room, plugging in lights but taking care not to have any of them suddenly flash on. All of Brenda's focus was on Emily's face. She had a halogen natural light makeup lamp with her, and years of experience taught her that this was the best light to do someone's makeup so that whoever was watching on the screen at the other end of the broadcast would get the most fetching version of her subject. Emily was about five years younger than Brenda, but they were worlds apart in every other way. Brenda was an urban sophisticate, well read, well travelled, and knew how to order wine in about seven or eight different languages. She kept her chestnut hair in loose curls, and the thickness of it framed her face and made her look like a movie star. Her lips were red and swollen, and her little chin and small nose made her greenish eyes stand out as if they were lit up from within. She wasn't naturally tall, but she was definitely curvy, and often had to wear platform heels to stand eye to eye with everyone else in a crowded room. Without her collection of giant shoes, she would only come up to everyone's chin, and people would wonder whom the munchkin was.

People as short as she was had an advantage of having a much more pronounced figure eight body shape, mostly because there wasn't much between the tops of their hips and their ribs, so all you could see when you looked at her was a thick tumble of dark, wavy hair, her almost comical pronounced facial features that made her look like a Vargas girl painted on the side of a B-17 bomber, then all of a sudden, just beneath her shoulders it was boobs, ribs, waist, hips, and curvy butt, and it was all compacted into about two feet. Beneath that there were about three feet of legs, then those giant shoes that made her stand to at least five foot eight, where she was comfortable looking at everyone. She carried herself so well and so confidently that no one would ever guess that she was less that five feet six inches, when she was really barely over five feet tall. It was all part of her execution of the person she portrayed herself to be, a sexual dynamo and a star, a giant in a male dominated world.

Emily was a beauty of different proportions, and Brenda was loving making her up and dressing her, which was going to come later. Emily was a bit taller and more natural looking, less curvy but more athletic, and her hair was a natural dishwater blonde that had summer streaks in it even during winter. Her greatest asset was her smile, which was real and hadn't been tainted by years of lies from boys and men and more years of asshole bosses trying to fuck her after everyone else had left the office for the night. Her eyes sparkled bright blue, and she could switch between prom queen sweet and track star glow in the blink of an eye, so Brenda played up on her natural oats and honey farm girl looks, keeping the rouge and lipstick to subdued colors and concentrating more on highlighting her cheekbones, her long neck, and her cute little ears, which Brenda loved making her giggle by using the camel hair brush on.

After she had the perfect face on, Brian slowly turned on a few lights and they moved her this way and that, trying to get the best lighting angle they could but still have it look like a hospital. They gave a guard an extra $50 to make sure NO ONE came near the room. All day long the phone had been ringing and reporters from all over had been trying to talk to Emily, but she had kept her mouth shut and wanted to tell her story only to Brenda. After they had the perfect makeup and lighting, Brenda nodded for Brian to step out for a minute so that she could dress Emily up in a wrapping of fabulousness that she brought special to make her look amazing, and the transformation from farm girl to sultry victim of passion was mesmerizing. Brenda helped her into a satin camisole, then pulled the cashmere sweater over her and adjusted her breasts so that they stood firm and proper, but not without giving them a little love and attention, just a quick hug and a kiss for each one, to let her know she had been thinking about them. Emily dug her nails into Brenda's arm to let her know this interview might go on a bit longer than expected, but at this point they were both hoping that was true.

After zipping up Emily in her skirt and moving her so that her legs and the slit of the skirt, her heels, the hospital bed behind her, and even an i.v. drip in her arm could be seen, Brenda looked at the masterpiece she had created and wondered how anyone could look at this girl on screen and doubt a single word she said.

"Are you ready?" Brenda knew how to prime someone for a heartfelt interview and had been prepping her, cheering her up and letting her know that she was her friend, and whatever traumatic events had occurred in the forest were long over. She was safe and amongst friends, and the story she told would help keep other girls safe from the hands of...whomever. Brian flicked the camera lights on, slowly at first so they wouldn't blind Emily, and Brenda sat next to her so that they would be in the shot together. They were recording on HD, so they could edit it to a split screen later, but having them sitting next to each other instead of facing each other made it more comfortable for victims of traumatic experiences, almost as if it were the reporter and the victim together against everyone else, and not the victim alone telling her story.

Brian brought the lights up to full brightness, did a quick check on the sound levels, and the little red light on the camera blinked on. "Ready when you are. Remember, this is tape, not live, so if you stutter or your thoughts don't come as fast as your speech, just take a breath and start over. We can edit the interview so that you don't make any mistakes, so relax and take your time, there's no hurry. And by the way, you look AMAZING. Both of you do. This is going to be an epic interview. Ready when you are, camera's rolling, so we're go in 3....2....1.....and......"

"Wait" Emily said, and Brenda stopped what she was about to say and sat there with her mouth open, hoping it was just a bathroom break or nerves, nothing unusual and they would start again. Emily stood still as a statue, and Brenda waited not breathing at all.

"I need to tell you what happened"

Brenda looked at Brian, who nodded that yes, the cameras were rolling, then back at Emily, confused, as if she wasn't aware the interview had just started. She started to open her mouth again to speak, when Emily interrupted her.

"No. First I need to tell you what happened. Off camera."

Brenda looked at Brian and said, "turn the camera off", and Brian turned off the little blinking red light. This was one of the oldest tricks in the book. The camera kept rolling, but everyone assumed that once the little red light was off, there was nothing being filmed, and that's when people really opened up. Emily looked at both of them, and in a scared little girl voice, said, "Can I trust you guys?" Brenda and Brian nodded yes simultaneously, and the camera rolled silently on.

CHAPTER NINE

"I need to tell you this before we put it on tape, because I'm not really sure what to say. I don't want people to think that I'm crazy, but there's something else."

Brenda and Brian looked at each other, and Brenda squeezed Emily's hand reassuringly and told her, "There's no hurry, honey. You take all the time you want. You've got me for the whole night, and it's up to you how you want to spend the time." She gave Emily a little wink, and Emily blushed, but instead of smiling, she stammered a little and tried to put her thoughts into words.

"There was someone out there. I was kidnapped. Well, rescued, actually. But I don't want them to get hurt, and if I tell the story exactly like it happened, there will be a thousand hunters combing the area, and the people who found me will have to run and hide, and chances are they'll get caught, and I don't want that to happen to them." Brenda held Emily's hand tight. They were getting to a part of the story that Brenda thought was probably very traumatic for Emily, but for once, she didn't know what to say. She had interviewed men who had seen their wives and children raped in front of their very eyes, soldiers who had seen their best friends blown apart, terrorists who felt the whole world should burn for cheating them in life, but the only time Brenda was moved to silence was when she was with someone so innocent, and all she wanted to do was to make sure they didn't hurt any more by reliving the experience, but it was also her job to get the story.

"Emily, you have to tell me who took you. Even if you became friends with them, people can't go around abducting girls in the middle of the forest. Don't you realize how dangerous it is to have people like that running around up there?"

"That's just it, though. They weren't people."

Brian and Brenda looked at each other, and Brian almost gave away their secret that the tape was rolling by checking the viewfinder out of habit, but quickly recovered by saying, "If you want me to start taping, let me know." Brenda gave him a SCALDING look, knowing that he almost blew what was shaping up to be a SPELLBINDING interview. Emily had already signed the disclaimer forms, and anything she said in that room LEGALLY belonged to the news agency, so if they got her story secretly on tape and then she refused to go on camera, everything they had she didn't know was taped was legally theirs. It was a dirty trick, and Brenda felt awful doing it, but she had to keep telling herself that nice girls finish last, and bad girls get to party at the embassy.

"Emily, WHO took care of you in the forest?"

"They weren't monsters. They were very gentle. People call them Sasquatch. I KNOW IT SOUNDS CRAZY! I wouldn't believe it myself, but it HAPPENED to ME!" Then she started crying, and Brenda put her arms around Emily. Brian took the opportunity while Emily was in Brenda's shoulders to check the framing in his viewfinder and get a quick visual level of the sound. Emily hadn't noticed that the lights had remained on, and hopefully she wouldn't say anything, so Brian just knelt down and looked at the ground, hoping to be as invisible as possible, wondering if Emily was out of her mind, hit her head on a rock too hard, or was covering up for someone else. Either way he knew enough to keep his mouth shut, and sat still as a statue.

Brenda let Emily sob on her shoulder for a minute, stroked her hair, and gently took her face in her hands. "Emily, you need to tell me the truth of what really happened. If you're covering for someone, believe me, I've heard it all, and nothing will make me think you're crazy, or cheap, or stupid, but if you tell me what really happened, then we can decide how to move forward with this. You know you have to tell the police something. Right now they're deciding whether to spend the money on combing the area looking for a psycho teen girl abductor, or a gang of drug dealers you're covering for, and you need to tell me right now. If there is someone out there that needs your help, the best way to help them is to tell me exactly what happened, and then I'll help you in ways you could never have imagined. I have connections at the state and federal levels, so if it was an escaped convict, or an illegal alien hiding out, or even if it was your father and you're trying to hide a love affair, I've heard it all, and nothing will surprise me, but you need to be honest with me, and I promise to help you and whoever is out there you're trying to cover for."

"Promise?" Emily's face was streaked black with mascara, and Brenda could tell she was afraid. "Of course I promise." Emily sniffled a bit but then started talking. "I wasn't joking. There is a tribe of people...well, not really PEOPLE, but, kind of ....I don't even know, they could

PASS for people sometimes, I guess, but what people who live in the cities know them as Bigfoot."

Brenda stopped for a minute and stared at Emily. Just now she started to realize that maybe she wasn't kidding. Maybe she wasn't trying to cover for someone, and Brenda sat there with her mouth open trying to figure out what to say, but then Emily went on.

"They're really gentle creatures. They would never hurt anyone. They thought I was injured when I was camping. See, My boyfriend and I went for a camping trip to our usual spot, on the North side of Hudson Bay in the Quebec side. It's called the D'Ungava Peninsula, and it's really beautiful there. There are thousands of miles of rivers and lakes and they're all interconnected, especially in springtime when the snow melts and the runoff swells all of the estuaries. We went much farther than usual, but we had just gotten our grades back from term and we wanted to celebrate because we both did really well. We grabbed about a week's worth of food, our camping gear, some fishing stuff, and just planned on getting as lost and as far away from everyone as we could. Every time we go up there we dare each other to see how far into the forest we're willing to go, how far up the rivers we're willing to explore, and this time we brought along a ton of liquor and kept going farther and farther north. We always carry our GPS with us, and we try to stay within a few miles of the bay so we can't get permanently lost, and we got as far north as Puvirnituq Bay, but we just rowed up the river there that goes inland and kept going and going until there wasn't a light anywhere or any sign of civilization even at night. We kind of like it like that sometimes, knowing that no one can get hold of you, that you've got the forest all to yourself, but what we didn't know was that we were being watched. We got really drunk and passed out sleeping under the stars. I was having my period, so we weren't having sex, but the wolves could smell the blood. They were circling our camp, a whole pack of them, and if these. ...people....didn't come along, we would have been eaten for sure. They knocked Ethan out and zipped him up in the tent, building up the fire so the wolves wouldn't come after him, but they could smell the blood on me as easily as the wolves could, and the wolves thought I was an injured animal, and that's when they attack. The bloodlust makes them crazy, and they can't stop themselves. So really they saved my life. You're hurting me."

Brenda realized she had been gripping Emily's hand so fiercely that her nails were digging into her flesh, and she quickly let go, embarrassed that she had forgotten her ladylike manners. They both gave a little giggle, so Brenda knew she was forgiven, but stared at Emily without speaking and silently urged her to go on.

"They're really tall, and they have hair all over them, but they look more like Hagrid from "Harry Potter" than apes or monsters. They've been roaming in the wild, I guess forever, but they're such a small tribe, and so scattered, that they've been able to stay hidden all these years. The other thing is that if you shaved them, they'd look almost completely human. They can't talk like we can, but they're very intelligent and had their whole history painted on the walls of a cave they took me to. I could tell they were talking to each other, it wasn't grunting and groaning like people say, but it was more like another language, chuffs and moans, like Chewbacca. They also sang the most beautiful songs to me, and sat with me while I recovered from I guess it was shock, but I was so scared from the shock and being carried into the deep woods by these enormous creatures that I was comatose for I guess a few days."

"While they treated me, fed me, and sang to me, I slowly came to realize I wasn't going to be anyone's dinner, and started to relax. I looked on the paintings on the walls, and I could tell several of them had been shot by hunters over the last hundred years or so, but then they were dressed in people clothes and I guess they were classified as hunting accidents. That's why no one has ever captured one. I guess several have been shot, but once they got a close look at them and figured they could pass for human, people got scared to say that they shot at this guy because they thought he was a bigfoot, so instead of going to jail, they'd throw some clothes on him, and tell everyone it was a hunting accident. The police and natives in this and other areas from what I could tell have always known about these people, and have pretty much left them alone."

"I guess they used to be a bigger tribe before the French furriers and trappers came into the area. They brought guns with them, and even though the Bigfoot people had what they figured were rights to the land, and didn't want their kids stepping in those steel jaws that would take someone's leg off, they tried to scare the French away, but that only made them hunt them farther into the forest, or killed off as many as they could so they could go on trapping and killing for the ermine, beaver, and mink pelts that were so abundant in these areas. So the Bigfoot people were left with only a few scattered tribes throughout Northern Canada, and I guess that's what those other things are, Yetis and whatever in the forests of Russia or Tibet or wherever, and there have been enough explorers and drillers and hunters that no one who lives in those areas and knows how gentle these things really are wanted them hunted to extinction, so whenever anyone asks about them, they just tell them its legend. But PLEASE don't tell anyone they're up there! Brenda, if you put this on the news, the whole PLACE will be over run with hunters and trappers, there are SO many people who want to capture one of them alive, it would just destroy them. They saved my life…. and…. one of them…" Emily looked around the room as Brian and Brenda sat spellbound, not sure whether to continue or not. Brenda gave her a slow nod to go on, even though she was barely able to breath at this point.

"One of them…I guess…I guess he kind of fell in love with me." Brian almost fell over, and Brenda's mouth opened to the floor, and her eyes got as wide as dinner plates. She looked over at Brian, silently saying, "ARE YOU GETTING THIS?!?!", and Brian, who after YEARS of working on stories with Brenda could read her mind, thought back to her telepathically "YOU'RE GOD DAMNED RIGHT I'M GETTING THIS!" They both turned back to Emily, who was sniffling again and staring at the floor.

"They're really beautiful creatures. They're not all scary and matted like they look in pictures you see on television and whatnot. One of them had brown and white stripes like a deer, and his coat was just soooo beautiful, oh, my god, he was just gorgeous. And one of the females, well she was sooo soft, like a rabbit, and her hair was longer and shaggier, but it was still her winter coat I think, but I slept next to her many nights, and she was as warm and cozy as a big heated fur coat, and she was grey with white trim and had little flecks of black and you could see her skin through the fur, it was peach white, like your color a bit Brian, and again, if you shaved her, she would have been a gorgeous woman without all the fur, but WITH it, she was STUNNING."

"They even had a little baby Bigfoot and he was SOOOOO cute! He had big black eyes like a squirrel, but his face was kind of like a little spider monkey, and he was dark brown too, but he was a little more shaggy, but I think that's just because he was kind of a scamp, and his momma had to hold him down and lick him clean a few times a day as he squirmed and wanted to get away to come and play with me and I loved him SOOO much! It was like having a little furry boy who wanted to be with you night and day, and he followed me around like a little puppy, OH I NEVER WANTED TO LEAVE! " Now Emily was beaming, and once again Brian and Brenda read each other's thoughts (We HAVE to get out to that cave). They knew better than to let Emily know what they were thinking, and smiled and laughed along with her as the camera rolled silently along. Brenda caught herself thinking, "If even a LITTLE bit of what this chick is telling me is true, this is going to be the story of the century."

CHAPTER TEN

The mood of the room was visibly changed, and everyone was smiling and laughing at Emily's sweet story. Brenda had never let go of her hand, and Brian had never let her know that the camera was secretly rolling. Emily was all sniffles and giggling now, and seemed to breathing a sigh of relief, so Brenda asked a few loaded questions.

"So, you think if you tell this story on film, and we play it one the news or write it in the paper, you'll be endangering the lives of the creatures that were so nice to you, these, what were they, like Teletubbies?" They all laughed heartily and Emily screamed with delight. "NOOO! No, they weren't THAT silly!" They were all laughing so hard they could be heard outside, and Brenda shushed them all while they were still giggling. Hospitals are notorious for nosey nurses wanting everything as quiet as a library, and Brenda didn't want ANYONE even hearing one BIT of what they were talking about. She even thought better of it and checked outside the door to see if there were any police or family members still hanging around. If just ONE person heard any of this story and believed it, they would be up in those woods so fast with a posse of gun slinging money hungry cryptozoologists it would be impossible to stop.

Emily quieted down, but it felt good to laugh that hard for all of them. It had been a stressful few days, travel always makes Brenda need to relax, but the royal fucking that Brian had given her earlier was the best respite she could prescribe for herself. Well, she didn't want to get hooked on oxycontins again, so sex it was.

"Yeah, I guess that's basically it. If people knew they were up there right now, I mean, the locals know about them, but they don't want people nosing up around in their land either, that's why they all live up there, because no one comes up there except for National Geographic and a few campers, and they're no threat to them. Even if someone DOES see them, and it happens ALL the time, when they come back to town with an "I SAW A BIGFOOT!" story, they all get laughed at. The few people who have come back up there with a group of photographers or hunters have been met by the local sheriff, or the local tribe of Natives, who make sure no one comes around shooting up the place, they got kids too, and no one wants their kid getting shot by some Bigfoot hungry psycho with a shotgun. They keep a pretty tight grip on the place. Even my boyfriend and I had to sneak in the estuary to get upriver in our canoe in the middle of the night. They're not really looking for campers in small groups like us, but if more than two people came around with big equipment or gun cases then they can spot them right away. There's enough Native blood up there that they can find groups of people, even strangers with cameras get found out pretty quick, and sometimes they just get all territorial about the white man coming on their land and scare people off. I guess it's worked so far, but they're keeping a close eye on me. I didn't want to go and they didn't want me to, but if I didn't then people would have come around looking for me, and then they would have found them."

Brenda and Brian looked at each other, not really sure what to believe, but as long as they had Emily talking and the camera still secretly rolling, she wanted as much as Emily was going to tell in detail, whether it was made up or not. "You mentioned that one of them was in 'love ' with you. Can you tell me a little about that?" Emily blushed and looked at the floor, and stammered a few times, too shy to say what she wanted to. "I... I ...can we, maybe just...well, I mean.... can maybe I tell you, and then you tell Brian? Would you be mad if we did it that way?" Brenda looked at Brian who was already up and ready to head out the door. "Don't even worry about it Emily. It's part of my job, and sometimes there are things that are just private, and that's okay, but for being understanding I get a kiss." "OH, puh-LEASE!" Brenda blurted out, trying to be funny but she could tell Brian was a little jealous that she was getting the best parts of Emily. Brenda was sure he wanted to get in a little three-way action. She told him about fucking Emily in the Hospital on the way to the hotel, the whole time feeling how hard his dick was getting while he tried not to wreck another rental car.

Emily was more than enthusiastic about it, and said, "SURE Romeo! C'mere!" Brian gave Brenda a quick little smirk and she stuck out her tongue at him. Emily gave him a playful little peck on the lips, but it was just enough to be 'more than friends'. Brian raised his eyebrows and said, "How lucky I am to be in the company of two such amazingly beautiful and elegant women. I must have pleased the gods this week."

"What a CHARMER!" Emily giggled. "What a CROCK!" Brenda sniggered, and they all laughed a bit. Brian took a bow upon exiting, tenderly touching the place where Emily had kissed him, and asked if either if them needed a coffee, to which they both said yes, and he was out the door.

"So are you guys.....?"

"Brian? Well, he's my camera and sound guy, the best there is. We try to keep it professional."

"Yeah, but he's HOT. Come on, there's no way you two can be out on assignments together, stuck on hotels for days on end, and NOT be slicing off each other a little, hmmm? God, I'd KILL to be stuck in some city with nothing to do but him for three days. Tell me you didn't take him back to the hotel and fuck him after you fucked me. Ahhhh, I KNEW IT!" Brenda was blushing, something she tried not to do, but Emily bringing up the memory of the two of them getting wet and slippery all over each other's bodies made her breath a little heavier.

"I know I'm kind of shit in bed, but I've never been with a woman before, and I didn't know how to.... um, make you happy, I'm sorry.."

GOD she was SOO cute! Brenda was SMITTEN with this little bundle of freshman college girl energy, everything with her was puppies and butterflies, even her little undies had care bears on them with little pink bows, and Brenda was starting to get wet thinking about getting Emily dressed for the interview. She knew Emily put those little undies on just for her, she knew Brenda would be checking her out, and her matching bra that looked like it was freshly washed and smelled like Bounce, little things that girls love and Emily knew it and Brenda knew it, and they weren't done with each other just yet. Brenda tried to be professional as Emily lifted her leg so that the slit on the skirt slipped up and a little white peek of her underwear showed itself, totally by accident, to Brenda's hungry eyes. Brenda knew Emily was trying to seduce her. She had tasted blood and wanted more. All Brenda was trying to figure out was if Emily sent Brian out to tell her the rest of the story, or to try to get her clothes off again...

"You're naughty" Brenda coyly meowed at Emily, who was grinning from ear to ear, running her hand up Brenda's skirt. "I just want to know what it tastes like" Emily was being the aggressor, and Brenda loved it. Plus the fact that Brian or anyone else could walk in with coffee or a thermometer at any second turned both of them on in a bad way, but Brenda couldn't believe what a hungry little bad girl Emily was showing herself to be. Brenda let Emily lift up her loose blue skirt, the perfect complement to Emily's outfit. Brenda had to think about what they were going to look like in the interview and OH SHIT! THE CAMERA WAS STILL ROLLING! Brenda let out a more than stifled laugh, and Emily gave her a "What?" look. Brenda just said, "Oh, I'm just LOVING this side of you! I NEVER would have guessed!"

"Neither would I" Emily sexed back at her, letting her hand run to the top of Brenda's thighs. Brenda leaned back into the chair and spread her legs, and Emily looked up at Brenda with kittenish eyes, licking the insides of her thighs and fingering the middle of Brenda's panties, light blue that matched her dress, and more than a little wet. Emily took control, kissing and licking at the wet spot on the soft fabric and pushed hard with her face to really let Brenda feel her tongue through the fabric. Emily could taste the wetness coming through in hot and juicy dampness, then grabbed Brenda's panties and pulled on them so that they tightened up on her pussy, rubbing against her clit making her want to get fucked by this girl's mouth so bad that she sunk deeper in the chair, spreading her legs as far as she could and pulling her calves up by her ears, giving Emily full access to her steaming wet pussy, praying Emily was going to tear her panties off and go full on sucking her pussy until she came, which should take about ten seconds judging by how fucking turned on she was.

Emily pulled and tied her hair expertly back in one swift motion, Brenda was sure from getting it out of the way of countless blowjobs...All bad girls had that motion down. Once she flicked all of her hair on top of her head in a knot, Emily pulled the sides of Brenda's blue satin panties aside, exposing her dripping wet shaved pussy, dying for attention and throbbing with juice, ready to explode all over Emily's face. Brenda looked down at her, grabbed her hair by the knot on top and SHOVED her face into her pussy, her heavy breathing had turned into a chorus of moaning, and watching this big chested blonde girl work her tight little cunt was too fucking much. She grabbed Emily's tits through her shirt with one hand, and with the other grabbed three of Emily's fingers and shoved them inside her tight, hot little pussy, giving them a little flick to check the sharpness and length of Emily's fingernails, something she had to make sure to always do but within a second she knew they were satisfactory and unlikely to be fatal. Emily took the lead and bent over so she was on her knees and Brenda was tucked into the chair, her ass about to fall off the seat and her legs spread and up in the air. Emily's shoulders rammed right up against Brenda's thighs, stopping her from sliding down any further and kept rubbing her now dripping wet fingers inside her, looked up at this delicious brunette who had one hand inside of her dress, tightly pinching the nipple of her left breast and squeezing it hard while feeling up Emily with her other hand. Emily bent down and placed her mouth over Brenda's swollen clit and sucked HARD, licking and swirling her tongue in circles while applying pressure on the lower part of Brenda's tight little hole with her finger. Brenda gasped HARD and squeezed hers and Emily's breasts harder, pulling on the fabric of the gorgeous beige sweater she KNEW Emily's tits would look SO GOOD in, and almost ripped the fabric pulling it up so she could see Emily's round tits and fully pointed nipples, grabbing one of them and moving Emily's mouth aside, rubbed the nipple against her clit in a circular motion while Emily continued to finger her.

They both had their mouths open in ecstasy, and Brenda leaned over as much as she could and pulled Emily's mouth to hers so their tongues could slide over each other, licking and tasting her own pussy and driving herself crazy with the smell of sex. Emily lifted up the rest of her tight sweater so her tits were fully exposed, and Brenda grabbed both of them and sat up to fully enjoy them in her mouth. She licked and bit playfully at Emily's nipples and rubbed the whole of them all over her face, loving the female goddess she had seduced and was quickly falling for. Emily lifted up her tits with her hands then pulled on Brenda's hair from the back of her neck, playfully commanding her to suck those gorgeous tits, licking and sucking Emily's nipples and covering them with lipstick.

Emily then bent over Brenda to finish what she had started. She pulled off her sweater so that Brenda could watch Emily's breasts swell and roll while she moved up and down on Brenda's pussy, which was now dripping and throbbing, wanting Emily's tongue back on it. Emily was more than happy to oblige, and lifted Brenda's hips back up so that her legs were over Emily's shoulders and Emily had easy access to Brenda's sex...She loved looking at it, she had only ever seen another woman's pussy close up in magazines, and loved the way Brenda's was shaved around the sides and had a little 'porn patch' on top. She also loved the way it smelled, driving her crazy with lust and dying to satisfy this woman who had deflowered her earlier in the day. Emily dove back on Brenda's pussy lips with her tongue, rolling and sucking with her mouth and Brenda was COMPLETELY at her mercy, pulling her face in closer and harder on her sex and running her fingers through Emily's hair. Emily started the motion, and with Brenda moving her hips back and forth in the chair it only took a few seconds for them to lock into a buildup. Emily sucked and sucked every time Brenda's clit moved up and over her face, up and down, up and down, Brenda moaning "OOHHHHH!!! UUUNHHHH!!!" and going faster and faster, Emily now with her tongue all the way out and Brenda bucking her hips HARD against the chair, screaming "MMMMMMMHHHH!!! UUUUUUUOOOOOHHHH!!!!!" But muffling it in Emily's sweater which she had picked up and stuffed in her mouth to stifle the noise to keep the entire hospital wing from hearing them. Emily felt the gush of hot fluid coming out of Brenda's tight hole, and knew she was about to explode and took two fingers and DROVE them deep inside of her, placing one on the outside of Brenda's ass and pushed HARD, driving Brenda INSANE and started her bucking her hips like a bronco at a rodeo, screaming into Emily's sweater "MMMMMOHHHH!!! NNNNNNNNHHHHH" and moving her hips up and down, up and down, and finally Emily SHOVED her tongue as DEEP into Brenda's hole as she could, Brenda screamed "HHHHHHHHHMMMMMMMMMMMMMMM!!!!!!!!!!!!!!!!" and held Emily's head FIRMLY pressed against her pussy, both of them holding still but Brenda's pussy PULSING and throbbing, neither of them moving but Emily could FEEL the heat and pressure inside of Brenda's pussy with her fingers, Brenda shoving down on the finger pressed up against her ass, and her whole body was one electrically charged pressure point, every muscle flexed and every hair standing on edge as she pulsed and shivered into a mass of pleasure.

After about fifteen seconds of staying perfectly still and enjoying EVERY bit of her climax, Brenda let go of the back of Emily's head, which she realized she was trying to shove inside of her. Emily gave Brenda's pussy a quick kiss, and rubbed her face into it giving the clit a quick lick making Brenda jump and throb again, going "MMMMmmmmmmhhmmmm" and smiling up at Brenda, who was looking down at Emily in amazement. Neither of them knew what to say, which was RARE for Brenda, because SHE was usually the one in charge of her sexual conquests, and NEVER had she had one turn it around on her so quickly, and do it so WELL. They relaxed and get dressed, making little "WHEW!" noises and giggling at each other.

Brian was either listening at the door waiting for the appropriate time to make his re-appearance or just happened to get back the second they finished dressing, which was highly unlikely. Brenda was sure he had come back earlier but was too smart to walk in on them like that and ruin it.... Brian knew her well enough to listen at the door before barging in on and interview subject, even if he was expected. If Brenda needed him, she would text and he was always close by. "Thanks" they both said as Brian handed them cups of gourmet steaming hot coffee. "Actually, Brian, could you give us a few more minutes? Emily and I need to discuss a few more points about what she is going to disclose to us, and as soon as that's finalized, we'll need you to finish the interview". Emily was thinking to herself, "We'll need full disclosure on your dick if I get invited back to the hotel after we finish this" and smiled discreetly. Brian smiled at them and left without giving Brenda 'that look' which meant he knew what they were up to. He was much too classy to be doing high school moves like that.

"Well, I guess I should thank you for that little...interlude. Ummm, I though you said you had never been with a woman before, was I right or did I hear you wrong? Because YOU were AMAZING." Brenda might say things like that to stupid guys who ALWAYS wanted to hear how good they were, but she was being sincere on this one.

"No, really! This was my first time with a woman. Well, my second, if you count earlier today. I've always thought about it, but when you live in a small town, EVERYONE knows your business, sometimes even before you tell anyone. People know your car, see where it's parked in the morning, know who you were with the night before, see who you leave a bar with, so there's no chance for any privacy. I've always wanted to live in a big city where you can be COMPLETELY anonymous, and you can be someone different every night."

"Well, it might SOUND great, but sometimes I wished I lived in a place where I had more people around who really knew me, not just a bunch of anonymous assholes. I guess the grass is always greener, huh? But I'd LOVE to have you come stay with me in L.A. sometime soon. We could hit the Hollywood parties, and I'll take you to a premier or some fancy nightclub where everyone will think you're a starlet in the making. Girls always go out as couples in L.A. and even if they're not together they act like they are. They get more attention from guys that way, and if the two of US went out? WHOOO! The WHOLE town would be begging us to be sitting at their table!"

"THAT sounds like a LOT of fun! Can we really do that? Or are you not going to call me again after you leave?" Emily was making a pouty face that let Brenda know she was half joking. She was a sweet girl, but she was also smart enough to know that people break promises to brand new lovers.

"Tell you what. Let's finish this interview, and then if you want, I'll email the footage to Mel, my boss, and if it's something they want, we'll fly you out to Los Angeles to do the interview. How does that sound?"

"When? You mean like soon?"

"I mean like tomorrow! If what you're telling me is true, then I'll get this approved, and you'll be on a plane to Los Angeles in about twelve hours. How does that sound?"

CHAPTER ELEVEN

Emily BEAMED with pleasure, but then her smile quickly faded. Brenda could almost see her story slipping away second by second, and she knew that Emily was either a VERY CLEVER attention seeking con artist, a SEVERELY traumatized kidnap victim, or the third possibility, that there really were bigfoots in the forest, and Brenda HAD to find out which one it was before making any kind of decision. Brenda put on her serious face, and tried to think analytically for a second. This girl CLEARLY knew she had Brenda wrapped around her little finger, and Brenda NEVER let anyone, ESPECIALLY an interview subject, have the upper hand. If they wanted to look good to the world, they had to PAY for it. Brenda had that kind of power.

She ALSO had the power to make you look shady, stupid, power hungry, impudent, greedy, in fact, Brenda was so good at choosing her words and her questions with lightning speed from one second to the next that she could either destroy a person's career or make them a superstar in the space of about five minutes. She was so good at it that there were often envelopes left in her mailbox the day before she was to go on the air with a very influential person, and these envelopes contained American Express gift cards in them for tens of thousands of dollars. There was never a name on the card, nor a return address, so who could ever prove where it came from or who sent it?

It was how the wheels were greased, and she only took them if she was ALREADY going to help that person along. She knew well in advance if she liked what they were doing or was going to expose their mischief, and when someone tried to buy out her silence, she dropped the 'gift card' back on the floor of the green room where the guest was before they went on the air. That's how they knew they were in trouble. Brenda always called it her 'fair warning' signal. She had a thing about not attacking someone who thought they were going to get off easy, and that was her way of letting them know to be prepared, but for the most part they already knew their career was over, and all they could do was try and control as much of the damage as it was going to cause them.

SO what to do with miss college nature girl here? Brenda loved her hot little body and the way she purred and responded to her affection. There was something about her that couldn't be put into words, she was just.... different. But was she bullshitting to cover for someone, or did she just not want to tell the truth, or WHAT the fuck was going on? Brenda realized she had been SO wound up in this girl's tears and dressing her in pretty clothes that she COMPLETELY felt taken in, and this was all a big lie to get a free trip to SOMEwhere. I guess this girl loved traveling, and after going missing she figured that someone was going to want her on air somewhere, all she had to do was pick which website or station was going to fly her out. Suddenly Brenda snapped into reality.

"Okay, so darling, we are running short of time. I need to know the rest of the story before we decide if you should go on camera or not, okay?" The camera that had been rolling OH SHIT! Brenda quickly started almost hyperventilating, thinking, "I've GOT to get the footage of this girl fucking me out of the camera before anyone sees it!" Brenda let out a little gasp of a laugh to herself, and Emily gave her a 'what's so funny? look, then decided whatever it was, her story was more important at the moment.

"Well, like I said, at first they took me to save me from the wolves. They carried me into the forest, and I was still stinking drunk, so when they carried me my head was upside down and I blacked out. I don't even really remember them saving me, but I DO remember the wolves, their glowing eyes just outside of the circle of firelight, and trying to wake my boyfriend up. I couldn't really stand up, we had smoked some really potent herb, and if you're really drunk, that's the LAST thing you should do, because it sends your already out of control body into a spin that you can't recover from.

When I woke up the next day, I was in the back of a dark cave, and naturally I was terrified. I couldn't see too well at all, but I knew that SOMEONE was there. I could hear what I thought were people at first moving around in the cave near me. There was just enough light that I could see what direction the entrance to the cave was in, so we had to be a good seventy to one hundred feet back. I've been in enough caves to know how light travels inside them, but I still couldn't see who was in there with me. I was frozen with fear. I was laying on something matted and hairy, and at first I thought it was an old sheepskin rug, but then I could feel it BREATHE! I almost screamed and started to sit up and try to see in the dim light, but all I could make out were where the sides of the cave were.

When I sat up the thing I was on top of MOVED again, and I scrambled to get away from it. Now I thought I was in a BEAR cave. I thought, what else could be so big and hairy? I sure as hell wasn't laying next to no fucking MOOSE." Brenda giggled and Emily giggled back, not having even realized she had even said anything funny.

"So I was scared out of my mind, I couldn't see, I had NO idea where I was or where Evan was, I didn't know what day it was or how long I had been out, and now I was stashed in the cave to be some Grizzly bear's lunch. I just started thinking about seeing my little sister again, and how I HAD to survive this. Slowly I started feeling my way around the floor of the cave. Let me tell you there were some things on the floor which made me SURE this wasn't some camper's lodge. I could feel bones and what felt like hardened shit and some other squishy stuff that just didn't belong where people do. I was POSITIVE at this point I was in some kind of animal lair."

"I kept crawling towards the light and came up to a bend. I peeked around the corner and I could see a straight tunnel that led to an exit where there was daylight. I could see vegetation, vines and moss all over the front so I'm sure it would be invisible if you were looking from the outside. I could see movement, but I HAD to get out of there before something decided to eat me or realized I was trying to escape, and there was only ONE way out. As I crawled towards the exit, I could see that the movement was only a fawn, a brown and white striped deer that was probably just foraging. I didn't want to disturb it because the bears or whatever would come wanting to kill it if they heard it, so I crept up to it quietly, hoping it would just dart away when I got close enough.

When I was almost near the entrance, I could see the deer through the hanging vegetation but it didn't know I was there. I didn't want to scare it, so I made a "ssst" noise trying to get it to run away. But it didn't run away. It stood up. That's when I realized this thing wasn't a deer at all. It had short brown fur and white stripes, but when it stood up, it was about seven feet tall, and looked like a human, a human with fur. It looked back into the cave at me and Brenda, I screamed the most BLOODCURDLING scream I ever have in my life. I can almost positively say I wet myself, and the blood rushed to my head so quickly that I passed out again."

"When I woke up, I was back in the cave again. I could hear water dripping, and I was SO thirsty from being drunk and everything else, and I knew that in survival situations the MOST important thing is clean water, so I searched for the dripping sound. I felt a hand gently close around my arm, and guide it to a bowl on the ground. It dipped my finger in the bowl, and it felt like water. I lifted the bowl, which felt like hardened clay, up to my nose and smelled. Other than the odor of the cave, which was musty and not pleasant, but not horrible either, I couldn't smell anything in the bowl, which was a good sign. I dipped my finger in and place a drop on my tongue, and again, it tasted like clean water. I took a sip and swished it around my mouth, and it still tasted clean, so I swallowed. There was no aftertaste, no discernable odor or 'coloring', which would mean stagnant water or some kind of 'knock out' drops. I was still terrified and didn't know where I was or who was in the cave with me or WHAT THE FUCK was that THING that stood up outside the cave, but I had to have water or death was sure to come quickly. I drank the whole bowl, and I could hear it being refilled for me. I drank again, and wondered whether to speak or wait. I decided to speak."

"Thank you" I said, waiting for a reply. There wasn't one.

"Are you the person who saved me from the wolves?" Still no response.

"Do you know if my boyfriend is okay? The man I was with, did you help him too?" STILL no reply.

"WELL GOD DAMNIT SAY SOMETHING!" and I could tell the person took off towards the exit of the cave. Even though I couldn't see them, I guess I scared them a bit, but I was scared, too! I stood up and felt my head swim from a hangover and my balance was off from this and the darkness. I started towards the corner towards the exit. This was the only instinct I knew, go towards the light. It was dim, much more than before, and I knew it must have been getting dark, which meant I had slept the whole day away. I was SURE people must be looking for me by now, and I was wondering when I was going to hear gunshots. They fire off gunshots in the areas people are lost in so they can follow them back. They do this for at LEAST the first three or four days and nights, hoping to lead the person back towards a rescue."

"I peeked around the corner, and fuck me if I didn't see FOUR of those fucking things all standing by the entrance! I was sure I wasn't noticed, the corner was that far back from the opening that they wouldn't have heard me. I could see the one I saw earlier, plus one that had a long dark grey coat, another with a long black coat, another

111

with a light beige coat, and the were ALL very tall and had to stoop down to be inside the cave which I could EASILY stand straight up in. They were making noise, but they weren't talking, at least not in a language that I knew. It was like a cross between apes talking and maybe like native Jamaicans? I don't know if that's right but it sure wasn't English nor was it any dialect of Native Canadian that I had ever heard. I was frozen on the spot. I couldn't get past them, and as far as I knew, that was the only way out of the cave."

"I don't know why I thought this, too much television I guess, but I felt around in my pockets and found my lighter. I crept back around the corner where they couldn't see me and flicked the light. Oh my god, it was like Fred fuckin' Flintstone's apartment. There were stone knives and axes lying stacked against the wall, bones of every kind but not flecked with rotten meat, but polished and looked like they had been boiled to clean them off. There were furs of all different kinds all over the floor, and what looked like grain baskets with seeds of wheat in them, I'm not great on botany so I wasn't positive. There were even what looked like a few beeswax candles and black burn marks above them, and every INCH of the walls were painted. I grabbed some of the furs and the beeswax, tied strips around a bone the size of a miniature baseball bat, and covered the leather in the beeswax. I flicked the lighter once, and the whole torch blazed up with light."

"Suddenly I could see the whole cave lit up, and I could tell right away this was only the entrance to a MUCH LARGER cave system. There were openings with passages leading away from this main entrance, and about seven

112

pairs of EYES looking at me from all directions! There were giant stalagmites and stalactites with bats flying around in them, little furry creatures scurrying in the corners, and the bowl I had been drinking out of, along with twenty other bowls all littering the floor, were all scooped out skulls. I SCREAMED and was so startled I almost dropped the torch, which was my most VITAL lifeline right now, and I just fucking RAN. I turned the corner to the outside of the cave and ran screaming "AAAAAAAHHHHHHH!!!!!", hoping to scare them enough to let me go. They stood aside for me at the entrance, but they gave me a look that was more like, "You're WELCOME, you crazy bitch! Next time have someone ELSE save your life!", and for some reason, I KNEW that's what they were thinking! I was still so scared that I just tore as into the woods, having NO idea where I was or where I was going. I knew GENERALLY where I was, but without my GPS there was no way I could tell longitude so I couldn't get an exact bead on my location. I figure I could just start walking West and I'd come across Hudson Bay eventually, but to give you an idea of how big the peninsula I was on is, If I started walking West, the distance could be farther than the width of the state of Michigan, so I was in bad shape to start with. The ONLY thing I had with me was my lighter, and THAT was almost out."

"I was still hung over, running in the dark, terrified, hungry, cold, still in shock from seeing those...THINGS, and in fear of getting eaten, but I was SURE that I would hear the gunfire of the search party. Sometimes they even light off fireworks that can be seen for fifty miles or more from a hilltop view on a clear night. EVERYONE who lives in North Canada knows how NOT to get lost, and more importantly how to increase their chances of being found. It's one of the things you just learn as a kid growing up near large patches of wilderness. I decided the best thing to do was camp for the night and light a signal fire that a helicopter could see. That was easy enough, but then I had to gather enough wood for the rest of the night, and THAT took two hours. I had NO place to lay down, just the hard dirt, and bugs kept crawling all OVER me, buzzing in my ears, biting my legs ALL night, and I had to feed the fire every twenty minutes or it would have gone out. I didn't sleep a WINK."

"The next day wasn't any better. I found water, but there are microbes that can make you VERY sick in river water, but I had no choice, and no way to boil water, which is what we usually do. I drank running stream water, which looked clear, but about four hours later I knew I was in bad shape. I had diarrhea and I was still having my period, so you can imagine what kind of a mess THAT was, plus my stomach was cramping, the bugs were biting, I was more miserable than I ever had been in my life. I lit another fire, a BIG one, hoping that SOMEONE would see the smoke, but no one came. I had no better time trying to sleep THAT night, and by the third day, I was immobile. All I could do was get up to take sips of water, which I KNEW was going to kill me eventually, and gather logs for my fire. I hadn't slept, I was suffering from every kind of survival illness you could get, and I could walk for a week through that thick forest and STILL never find anyone, it would just end at a big lake, which I might have to travel south ANOTHER week before I found anyone, and I was going to be dead LONG before then. I knew the only way to survive was to save my strength and stay put. I was able to scrounge up some honey from

114

a hive I smoked out, and I meted some of the beeswax and used it as an insect repellant, which kind of worked. I still hadn't eaten, I was FILTHY, and all I could keep doing was adding wood to the fire."

"Then the worst thing that could have happened, happened. Well, I guess the worst would have been the wolves coming back to eat me, but they didn't. The third night, just as I was finally dozing off, I felt a few little sprinkles of rain. I promised God, "God, if you don't rain on me tonight, I SWEAR I will never do a bad thing as long as I live PLEASE God not tonight!" God was thinking about it, because for the next two hours all that fell were little sprinkles here and there- not enough to get me wet, but enough to keep me awake. And then after two hours, in the middle of the night, the sky opened up and it poured. I was soaked instantly, and my fire was out as well. I walked around in the rain, FREEZING, trying to find ANYWHERE I could get out of the rain but there was nothing to be found. This was when I started to get SERIOUSLY afraid that I wasn't going to make it out alive. I was still TERRIFIED those THINGS I had seen back at the cave were out here LOOKING for me, so every little sound I heard snapped my whole psyche into tension, and you can only live a little bit longer at that point."

"The rest of the night was the worst of my life. I DREAMED about being near a fire swatting bugs and mosquitoes which I thought was hell the first two nights, but which at this point would have been HEAVEN. I kept moving, trying to keep the blood going, but all I realized I was doing was walking in big circles and talking to myself. That's when I knew I was going to die. When morning came, the rain stopped, but everything was

SOAKING wet. I tried as best I could to tear some bark and wood into kindling strips, but my flint had gotten wet and I kept flicking my lighter to the point where the spring and little wheel just snapped off, leaving me with nothing. I started crying. I sat down, but my ass got soaked, I stood up, but my legs were numb with pain. You know how FREEZING it is just at dawn, and I found a rock to lie on, and I cried, and thought, 'this is it. I'm just going to die right here'."

I could see it getting brighter but I was still frozen, shivering and my teeth were chattering, and again there was no sleep. I was SO COLD, I don't EVER remember ANY winter being that cold. I think that my core temperature had dropped, which is what that means. Every winter I had been in, maybe my skin got cold, but I always kept my internal body temperature up. Anyway, after a few hours of shaking violently from the fever I now had, along with whatever dysentery I had picked up from the water, along with the low iron from my period, plus having the runs, I just wasn't going to live. I took out a piece of bark, grabbed a sharp rock and scrawled my name on it. I tucked it inside of my shirt so that when they found my body they would know who it was. That was all I could manage to do before the rays of the sun hit me square in the face and I passed out, I figured for the last time."

CHAPTER TWELVE

"When I woke up, I was in the same blackness of the cave, but something was different. I was wrapped up in something soft and warm, I could smell something delicious, like stew or roast chicken. It was still black when I opened my eyes, so I wasn't sure if I was dead or what the deal was, so I tried to sit up. Bad idea. My body was so weak from fighting off infection some of my muscle tissue had wasted away, and I was in great pain every time I moved. I guess the noise I made let someone know I was awake, because I felt a hand on the back of my head lift me up a little, and a bowl of water being brought to my lips. I sipped at it as best I could, then I could smell the broth being brought to my mouth. The hand lifted me up, and I wondered if I was drinking out of a skull again, but had no choice if I wanted to live, so I drank the soup. It was delicious, whatever it was. I finished the whole bowl right there, and instantly felt better."

"I knew I had been drifting in and out of consciousness for what seemed like at least a week. I knew I had been battling a fever, probably dementia, hypothermia, disorientation, dehydration, diarrhea, menstrual cramping, hunger, fright, shock, and was probably just inches from death. From what I could gather, those things had followed me, or had been watching me, knowing that they live too far away from people for me to find my way back on foot. There's no way I had been running for over three days and they just happened to come across me again, so I was starting to think that maybe they didn't want to eat me, but what the fuck were they? I had been in near total darkness the whole time I was there, so I wasn't even sure how long that was. The difference between night and day was slight, and I'm sure there were fires burning somewhere in the cave because it was warm even outside of the furs I was wrapped in, and the food was hot. I was thinking that maybe they kept the lights off so I wouldn't freak out again. I think they were a little insulted when I ran off last time, waving a bone torch like a madwoman and not even a 'thank you'."

Brenda giggled and so did Emily. If Emily was making this up on the spot, she sure as shit was as quick a woman as Brenda had ever met. To include this kind of detail in a story is what good investigators LOOK for to see if people are lying. Generally liars will include big details, like 'the car was blue', but people telling the truth will tell you, 'the car was more of a sparkly royal blue, but there was a rust spot on the rear bumper, but it had to be at least twenty years old. I couldn't tell you the make or model but it had weird stitching holding a white ragtop on, kind of a cross stitch in a row of twos, and the metal bracing that controlled the convertible roof was black and stuck out like giant black scissors with the tips rounded'. This was the kind of information Emily was giving, and everything about her journalistic training told Brenda that Emily was telling the truth. Plus Emily was being funny without TRYING to be funny. Every time she cracked Brenda up, Brenda laughed first, then Emily. People who make things up and insert little jokes in their stories will pause for effect to see if their jokes work, and Emily didn't do this. Brenda nodded for her to go on, so they both took a long pull from their coffee, blotted their faces with ladylike precision, and Emily took a deep breath and continued.

"I started to feel a little better, so I kind of sat up. Someone was always there beside me, and I felt a little pillow come under my back. Right then I noticed I had to go to the bathroom, so I asked, my voice still weak, "Can you show me where the bathroom is please?" and without hesitating, a hand grabbed mine, and I stood up and followed. I could hear little grunts and groans around me, and I knew I was surrounded by I think it was these things again. I was trying to be brave, but I was so confused, and it was so dark. I was wrapped up in furs, and for the first time I noticed that someone had taken my clothes off. At first I wondered if I had been sexually assaulted, but I think I might have remembered being violated. I seemed to more remember that I couldn't get up to use the bathroom, but someone had kept soft furs underneath me and cleaned me every once in awhile."

"The hand in the dark led me to a little enclosure that was maybe fifty or sixty feet from where I had been laying and I could hear water running. Just as I was wondering what was going on and where I was, I felt the hand put something in mine, and it was unmistakably a lighter. I flicked the light, and it was a zippo so it stayed lit. I was in a small room that was stone all around, but there was a little ledge just big enough to sit on with a hole in it. I looked in the hole, and that's where I could hear the running water. I was sure there was a stream or an underground aquifer running underneath it, but it had no discernable smell that an outdoor bathroom might. It wasn't covered with urine or fecal matter, and there was a small stack of rabbit pelts, cut into little squares all hanging on a stick that was on the wall. I remember thinking, 'Not even the nicest hotel I've been in had rabbit pelts for toilet paper!' And let me tell you, it's a treat for your butt you'll never forget."

At this Brenda BURST out laughing, and Emily followed again, not realizing how funny that was. Brenda had actually spit out half a sip of coffee, and was falling over laughing and trying to wipe it up but shaking from laughing so hard. There were actual tears forming in her eyes, and she laughed so hard she said she "I gotta go pee, do you have any rabbit pelts?" And they both fell over laughing. Brenda ran into the bathroom and continued laughing as she relieved herself and yelled out, "Hey! I'm outta rabbit pelts in here! Can you hand me some?" At which they both HOWLED with laughter. Brenda finished up and walked out, still sniffling and chuckling with Emily. She wiped away the tears that had formed when she laughed so hard, and handed Emily a clean tissue. "Please, go on!" Brenda said, trying to be serious, but they both still had the giggles at this point and went on for another thirty seconds trying to shake it off. Finally they calmed down and Emily was able to continue.

"When I got finished I saw a hand reach inside the room, and I noticed right away it was covered with fur on top, but the underside was like a white woman's hand, completely bald, which is what I felt when she led me around, and that's why I hadn't freaked out yet, but here was this hand reaching into the cave-bathroom, and I wasn't sure what to do. I flicked the lighter off because I was afraid to see her face. I also started to think that maybe this was some kind of a leper colony, or these people were victims of some disease or an experiment gone wrong and didn't want people pointing and poking at them. But I still wasn't sure they WERE people! I couldn't tell! No one had spoken to me and I was in near pitch dark, but they seemed to be able to understand me. Their skin under the fur seemed human, but the tops of them looked like, well they all looked different, but they looked like ANIMALS."

"I was scared, but started to feel like I wasn't in danger. If they WERE people there was something SERIOUSLY wrong with them, and if they WEREN'T people, how were they able to take care of me and know what I was saying? That's why I was so scared; I didn't know what I was dealing with. But for some reason I think they could sense that, and they were doing everything they could to keep me from being afraid. I'm sure if the lights were up I would have been screaming bloody murder and maybe would have hurt someone or myself. I think they knew that the dim light would give me time to adjust and realize that I wasn't in any danger, and I was starting to realize that these creatures had saved my life TWICE."

Just then Brian politely knocked and stuck his head in. Brenda was so entranced with what Emily was saying that she quickly turned her head around and before Brian could say anything, she just said, "No, we're fine, thanks. I'll call you in a few" and made a few compulsory *kiss kiss* noises, to which Brian's head immediately disappeared back out the door.

"Wow, you've really got him under control, huh?"

"Well, no, we've just been working together long enough to know how to read each other's minds, and if I was getting a better story by interviewing you myself, he knows it. If he was getting better material without ME around, he'd let me know and I'd be out of the room quicker than HE was, so it's a mutual respect thing." Brenda realized she should ask Brian about the time of the tape in the camera; if it was going to run out, it would make a bunch of R2-D2 noises and it would be pretty obvious that the tape had been running the whole time. If Brian was a smart cameraman, and he was, then there was at LEAST a fresh two-hour tape in the camera. The camera was plugged into the wall for this one, so there was no need to worry about the power going out, but they were at LEAST an hour into the tape and it hadn't shut off yet so it was either a ninety-minute cassette or two hours. Brenda reminded herself to ask Brian in about fifteen minutes, and then nodded for Emily to continue.

"So I started to realize that these things, whatever they were, had saved my life and been taking pretty good care of me. Plus I think that whatever was in that soup had a narcotic effect, because I was feeling REALLY good, kind of loopy and silly, you know that feeling, like if you take a couple of Vicodin?" Oh, yeah, Brenda knew that feeling all right. She nodded for Emily to go on. "Yeah, so I was suddenly realizing I was in a pretty funky mood, and I was feeling SO much better from nearly being dead not too long before. I started to get up, and I heard a roomful of things moving carefully around me, not making any sudden or loud noises, but aware that I was getting up and moving out of my way. I wrapped myself up in the fur blankets they had me sleeping in, and walked slowly towards the corner where I could get to the entrance. No one, or should I say no THING, I wasn't sure yet, tried to stop me or get in my way. In fact, the entire path to the entrance was open all the way to the outside."

"I slowly moved towards the exit realizing that they were all behind me, watching me and being very still. I had seen people act like this, like handlers at a zoo when they get a new animal. They don't want it scared so they move very quietly and slowly around it, and that's how I felt, except I was the animal and everyone was trying not to scare ME. I kept moving closer and closer towards the entrance to the cave, the light getting brighter and brighter all the time. I looked behind me, and I could see shapes, figures that looked like shoulders and heads, dark eyes and mouths, but they were still in the shadows and I couldn't really tell what they were. All I knew was that they weren't trying to stop me from leaving, and that made me feel safe. I crept closer and closer to the opening, until I was at the mouth of the cave and could touch the vine leaves that hung over it, smell the fragrant air and see the bright sunshine of the forest around us. I looked back and could barely see the creatures anymore, but I knew they were there and were watching me."

"I stepped outside of the cave, still wrapped in my furs and feeling the fresh air and sunshine. I kept walking slowly, but after a few feet I turned around and realized I couldn't see the cave entrance anymore. It was REALLY well hidden and on the side of a hill that you would just never suspect it was there. I kept walking, slowly, wondering if I should make a run for it, but I knew that after saving my life twice, why would I be in danger from them? Plus I was feeling good from the medicine in the soup, so I relaxed a little and sat on a log, wrapped in my furs to enjoy the feeling of the sunshine on my face and having gotten over my illness. I really thought I was going to die, and for a second I wondered if I hadn't actually died and this beautiful meadow I was in wasn't some transient place for my soul. But I quickly dismissed that as just my mind wandering and tried to think about where I could be. I knew I had walked west for about three days, so I HAD to be somewhere REALLY far from where I was camped because we had been on a tributary that connected to Hudson Bay, and I doubt that I had been carried off the peninsula because that would be at least three hundred miles."

"Just then I heard a noise behind me, so I turned around and at the entrance to the cave was...one of them, and he was standing holding the vines open as if they were drapes or a curtain he was holding back. He stepped the rest of the way through the entrance and stood there looking at me, and I wasn't sure if he was more curious about me, or I was more curious about HIM."

"How were you so sure it was a male right away?" Brenda asked, still totally entranced, but dead serious and starting to believe every word of it.

"Because he was covered with fur and had a thick shaggy beard, but looked like he could have just been a big hairy man, and if he were shaved all over, he could be just a big guy. But the reason I was sure was because..." And Emily leaned in to Brenda, who leaned in right back, "Because his cock was HUGE!" and Emily grinned a wicked grin. Brenda smiled and nodded, still wondering if this was bullshit or this girl was crazy, or what the fuck was going on.

"So I decided that these weren't people playing a joke, because if it was they would have put a LOT of effort into making these costumes and making the sex organs look real, as well as the eyes, the hair, EVERYTHING about them told me they were no joke and what I was seeing was real. Just then two more of them stepped out behind the first one, whom I guessed was the leader. One was female, and the other was almost as big as the first, but his fur was darker. They all had black eyes with some white around the outside but more like an animal's eyes than a person's, but there was another thing that made me stop dead in my tracks and realize who these might be."

Brenda could barely breathe. "Go on" she said, without even realizing she said it out loud.

"They all had ENORMOUS feet. I realized that what I was saved by, and had cared for me, what were people for hundreds of years had called 'sasquatch' and people now called 'bigfoot'. I KNOW that's impossible, right? But there they were, looking right at me. I was frozen on the spot. After the initial shock was over, the first thing I thought, which I'm now ashamed to admit, was, "I'm going to be a MILLIONAIRE!" The amount of money I could get for telling people where these things live, and PROVING they exist, would be ENORMOUS! But HOW could I do such a thing? After they had saved me, kept me alive, and allowed me to run free with no thought about kidnapping me, or holding me to make sure I didn't talk, that's not who I am."

"The first thing I wanted to do was to thank them for saving me. I guess I still hadn't decided if I wanted to stay or not, but I wanted to at least let them know I was grateful. If they could tell I wanted to go to the bathroom, they would be able to tell I was thanking them. I slowly walked back towards them until I was about ten feet from the cave entrance. I could see a few more of them behind the others, and they were all GORGEOUS. The one thing no one ever mentioned about these creatures was how BEAUTIFUL their coats were. I guess if they did, they would have been hunted to extinction a LONG time ago. Can you imagine some rich bitch in Manhattan going, "Honey, will you get my fur, no, not the mink, the BIGFOOT coat?" At this they both chuckled, sipped their coffee, and Brenda was quiet as a church mouse as Emily went on.

"I looked at them and they all looked at me, not like dinner, but you know how a family you've been visiting or relatives get together on the porch to say goodbye to you when you're leaving? It kind of felt like that. They were all very still and I said, "Thanks.... thank you for saving me and taking care of me". None of them said a word, nor did they seem confused by the sound I was making. They all just stood there, not moving at all. I wasn't sure what to do. I tried speaking again. I said, "Can you understand me?" and again I got no response. Just then, a female of the group came forward. She was no knuckle dragging ape relative. No, THIS girl sauntered like Jessica Rabbit, with AMAZINGLY clean white fur from head to toe. She looked like some kind of Mount Olympus goddess, and her face looked like a cat's. She had cat eyes, greenish brown, almost yellow in the middle, and a little triangle nose, with what looked like whiskers on her face. She was SO BEAUTIFUL I couldn't look away. For living in a cave in the woods, she was PURE white, as if she was brand new. Her hips swayed as she walked, and she had a supermodel's figure. I couldn't really see her..(and at this

Emily lowered her voice)...*pussy* , because it was all covered with short white fur, but her body was DEFINITELY female. Even her breasts were covered with short white fur, except for her (lowered her voice again) *nipples* , which were bald and pink. There were little parts of her tummy where her pink skin showed through, and her ears were pointed, but oh, was she something else!"

"She walked out of the cave and walked up to me. She was even more dazzling close up than she was far away, and I was JUST in awe of her. She DEFINITELY gave off the female vibe, and I could tell SHE wasn't that impressed with ME. I think it was because some of the other males had been staring at me VERY intently, and it just FELT like she was ready for me to leave. She held out her hand, and in it there was an animal skin bag. I took the bag from her, and in it were a lighter (the zippo I had been handed earlier), some dried beef of some kind, a compass, a flare gun, a silver survival blanket, and a few boxes of army food, you know, those MRE's they eat in the field? How in the FUCK did they know what these things were? Were they telling me to leave? Were they just offering to help if I DID want to leave? None of them still had said a word, so I said, "Thank you" to the female, and she looked at me with a look that said, "Don't let the door smack you in the ass on the way out" I SWEAR TO GOD!"

Brenda and Emily both started laughing at this, and just then the door knocked. It was Brian with two more cups of coffee, and he just set them down on the table and started to step out. "Just a second" Brenda called to him, and he turned around, "Yeah?" "Emily, I need to talk to Brian for a second, DO NOT MOVE A MUSCLE" Emily smiled, and Brenda decided to play up to her suspicions. Brenda grabbed Brian by the shirt collar and pulled him into the bathroom (it was a private hospital room, so it was in the room by the entrance) for a second, whispering, "was that a ninety minute tape or a two hour you put in the machine? If that thing shuts off and she knows it was running, we're DEAD!"

Brian looked at Brenda for a second, then at the floor, and said, "I can't remember"

"WHAT THE FUCK DO *what the fuck do you mean you can't remember?* That's your fucking JOB is to remember! You better remember RIGHT fucking NOW or so help me I'm going to fucking KILL you!"

"Well don't panic, I'll just say I need to borrow the camera for a second and just put a new two hour tape in and bring it back"

"AND WHAT, JUST HAPPEN TO SET IT UP FACING US *facing us the same as it was five minutes after you left? She may be blonde, but she's not a fucking RETARD! Brian, if that tape shuts off in fifteen minutes, you had BETTER hope you find a new job before I get hold of you, because if THIS story is blown because of you NOT remembering, I will have you BLACKLISTED all over the news world and you'll be filming weddings in New Jersey for the REST of your LIFE!"

Brian gulped. He knew she was just giving him a hard time, but weddings in New Jersey.........brrrrrr. He had told Brenda that's how he got his start in the video world, and he was originally from New Jersey. Videotaping New

Jersey weddings were the most thankless, horrific, humiliating job in the world, and there was nothing celebratory about them. He spent the whole wedding getting yelled at by the bride, then the groom, then the parents, then the friends and relatives, and no one EVER liked how they looked so they blamed it on HIM, and everyone tried to sue him for a refund. It was hell on earth. The tape that was in the camera was...FUCK! He couldn't remember. He looked in his bag for the empty, but there were tape cases of every configuration in there, and it could have been any one of them. "Well why don't we just pretend it's a ninety minute tape and I'll just get it out of the room now?"

"BECAUSE THIS IS THE INTERVIEW OF A LIFETIME YOU STUPID SHIT! AND IF *and if this gets blown because of you, *...JESUS, I need EVERY second of what she says! You have got about TEN minutes to figure this out, because if SHE'S not done talking and that machine goes off, YOU"RE DEAD. If you run in and grab the camera and STOP the tape BEFORE the interview is done and there's a half hour of film left in the camera, YOU'RE DEAD. GOT IT?!?! FIGURE IT OUT!" And at that she grabbed Brian by the hand and led him out of the bathroom smiling, and took him to the door to the room and gave him a bite on the check, though Brian knew it was a warning even though it looked like a kiss to Emily. "See you in a bit, handsome", Brenda winked at him, and Brian gulped again. She turned warmly back to Emily and smiled like a cat that was sitting on a mouse.

"Now, where were we?"

CHAPTER THIRTEEN

"I stood there at the cave entrance with all of them, this family of Bigfoot creatures, looking at me. They were obviously letting me go, but I couldn't tell if they WANTED me to go, or if they were just letting me know I could leave if I wanted to. The snow white female definitely wanted me to leave, and she had gone back into the cave after handing me the bag of supplies. The other ones just stared at me looking more like they were sorry to see me go. I guess when you save something you kind of have an attachment to it. I saved a baby bird when I was a little girl, and when it was healthy enough to fly away, I cried for days. That's all I could think of when I looked at them. I was their baby bird, and they were sad to see me go."

"I started to walk away, but then I kept thinking these creatures must really be sad to see me go. Over what must have been the last ten days, they had saved me from wild wolves, carried me God knows HOW far to their cave to keep me safe, and after I escaped, they followed me to make sure I got back safely, found me almost dead, and then for probably a week nursed me back to health, and I didn't remember ANY of it. All I remember was blacking out and being delirious with fever, and someone must have hand fed me, cleaned up if I peed, kept me wrapped in clean furs and even bathed me. I was sure this had to be a group effort; maybe they were so happy to see me well again and were really sad to see me go. I turned and realized I had been walking away from them, and when I turned back around, they had all walked back into the cave. That's when I started to cry."

"I lost all of my fear and started walking back. I had to let them know how I felt, and how grateful I was that they had saved me. When I got back to the entrance there was just one of them still there, and I realized that it was a female, a young one, and she had been watching me walk away, and watched me walk all the way back, but I noticed there were tears in her eyes as well. I was her baby bird, and she was so happy to see me well, but so sad to see me go, she was crying...We both looked at each other, she was probably still a child to them, she was only about four and a half feet tall with dark reddish hair, but we walked towards each other and gave each other the BIGGEST hug, oh Brenda it was something right out of a movie! She jabbered excitedly that I had come back...don't ask me how I knew what she said, I just did, because they all came running back to the outside of the cave, and next thing I knew, I had this family of furry, loving creatures all holding me and hugging and kissing me and some of them were crying and I was BAWLING. It was probably the most special moment I had with them. You never hear of a Bigfoot attacking a human, but I had no idea they were supposed to have had this depth of emotion, or been this close to people in their character."

"Anyway, one of the older females brought out a giant side of ribs I could smell cooking somewhere in the cave, and we all sat in the afternoon sun and had a feast. The little ones, they were SO CUTE! They had big black eyes, and they were all different colors, like different breeds of dogs, but they could have been human if they just shaved off the fur. But the little ones all wanted to touch me and play with me, and I could tell all week they had wanted to but the older ones shooed them away because I was so sick. So when I started roughhousing with them and playing catch with some toys they had and ticking them, it was like they WANTED me there, and they wanted me to stay with them! They all gave me that feeling, well, except for the furry white female, who had been nowhere to be seen since I returned. "

"After we finished eating, I sat with some of the adults and we drank more of their potion, I guess it was something they made special because I had never had it, and it sure felt good. Opium doesn't grow wild in Canada, does it?"

"Actually the *papaver somniferum* flower, also known as the poppy plant which produces opium, is indigenous to all continents except Antarctica, so it could really be found anywhere." Brenda loved showing off her encyclopedic knowledge of the world, but let Emily continue. Emily looked impressed but went on.

"Well we got pretty relaxed on this stuff, and after a bit, the sun started to go down. Not one of them said a single word I could understand, but I was sure they wanted me to feel welcome there. As it got darker the little ones came back out and pulled me inside the cave, guiding me by the hand in what to me was almost pitch black. They had ENORMOUS eyes, and my guess was that since their eyes glowed like cats do, they probably had incredible night vision and didn't need any light to see just fine in there, but I wanted to get to know more about my new friends. I flicked the lighter and found a few strips of leather and some beeswax to wrap around a bone, and then lit up a torch for the second time in there, but this time I wasn't afraid for my life."

"I could see where I had been laying on a pile of furs for... I wasn't sure how long, but I knew it was my bed. Next to it were bowls that probably had been used to feed me, and a pile of my old clothes. I felt so comfortable in the furs they made for me I forgot I must have looked like some wild cave woman. The bowls were still skulls though, and though I wasn't as afraid as before they still made the place look eerie. It wasn't very tall for a cave, but I could tell it was just the entrance, and the little ones pulled me toward what I could tell were more rooms behind this one."

"One of the passages led to the bathroom, or the rock seat with the hole, but it served its purpose, and they kept it clean. The other passages led to another cave, even bigger than the one in front. It looked like something out of a National Geographic magazine. There were Stone Age looking tools lying around and paintings on the walls and ceilings that seemed to go from one end to the other like a cartoon strip. As I got a closer look I could tell that's exactly what they were, and each painting told a different story. The little ones even pointed at paintings I could tell were of them, and squealed as if to say, "That's ME!" I pointed at the picture and then at them, and returned their excitement, which they loved and hugged me more. I could see that there were more of these Bigfoot creatures, probably another seven or eight in this room, and there were another two big caves that each held four or five more. Each time I entered the cave with the torch they all looked up at me, but continued what they were doing."

"Some of them were skinning furs off of animals, and the others were trimming the meat for cooking. The males seemed to be relaxing in their bedding that was just a pile of furs like mine was, but the females were tending to the young, cooking the food, even cutting up plants for food or that drink they made to get high. There were plenty of human made things in the cave; none of it being used for what is was made for. They had a big wheel kids' tricycle that they pushed food around with like a tray, there was a rifle that was used to hang skins on, a bicycle wheel was used like a grill, and the food was hung on the spokes and placed over the fire and rotated. It was actually pretty ingenious. No one I knew had a rotating grill, and here was one they made for free! They also had an IPAD in there, but the batteries were dead, so they used it as a tray to eat off of. I wondered what they had used it as before the batteries died, but I couldn't ask them."

"You also might think it was dirty and smelly in there, but it was actually really clean! There were furs all over the floor like carpeting, and they kept off of the dirt floor areas, or the floor was stone and they washed it off to keep it from getting dirty. They were also extremely well groomed. They preened and combed each other all day kind of like other animals do. I guess even we like having our back scratched or someone running their hands all over us, if it's the right person, I mean. There was even a water pool from the underground aquifer that they used for bathing, and they used some kind of moss looking stuff to keep themselves clean and they weren't smelly or filthy like you would think. They were such beautiful creatures, and if people found them, they would be the most incredible discovery since the new world."

"My torch ran low and the little ones walked me back to my fur lined bedding. By the time I was back there it was dark outside, but there were a few beeswax candles burning here and there so I could see what was going on around me. The little ones wanted to roll around with me and give me hugs, and when they were called by their, well, I guess it was their mothers, they whined and wanted to pull me with them to bed, Brenda, they were SO ADORABLE! They were just like little furry children, one of them had mottled fur, almost like camouflage or like a calico cat, all spotted white and brown and black, and he was SO soft! I just LOVED playing with them, they felt like giant rabbits, their mothers kept them so clean and their fur so shiny! They whined JUST like human kids do when it was time for bed, or a bath, but they were SO well behaved, I just loved them to death!"

"Then some of them went out of the cave I guess to hunt, and most of the others went into the back. There were about three I guess you could call them 'couples' that had bedding in the front room of the cave where I had my bedding, and they left me to wrap myself up in my furs and relax. The intoxicant they drank made you feel good just sitting there, but it also had another effect. Once I sat still and was relaxing in bed, I started to feel really aroused. I wasn't sure if it was the stuff I drank, or just because I was feeling better, but I wouldn't THINK this was the kind of place I would get horny, but I wasn't the only one. I could hear the others in their beds starting to fool around, and at first I wasn't sure that's what they were doing, but when I sat up to take a look at what they noise was, there was no doubt that they were all fucking each other! Every single one of the couples was mating, and it was some pretty hot action! I wasn't sure whether to turn around and give them their privacy because they sure didn't seem to care who saw them. The Males were REALLY hung, and other that having what amounted to fur for pubic hair, their dicks looked just like humans do. They seemed fur covered when walking around, but when they got hard, the fur pulled back like a foreskin and they looked normal."

"I was thinking about how they were probably related to us. I mean, ALL life forms on Earth are related, right? I mean, even people have like fifty percent of the DNA of a banana, isn't that right? So we MUST all be related. People have something like ninety-eight percent of the DNA of a chimp, so I was thinking we MUST have about ninety nine percent of the DNA shared with these things! I mean, they looked just like we do, only larger and with fur and giant feet. Chimps don't look anything like humans, well maybe compared to a jellyfish or something, but to humans, these things were WAY closer to us, and SO much more beautiful!"

"Anyway, they went on fucking for awhile, and then they all started to change partners! The females were the ones who climbed from bed to bed in a giant circle. First they went to one bed, and there were two of them in with one male, then the first one in that bed went to another bed, and so on, until they all went around the room at least twice! I was trying not to stare, but they didn't seem to mind me being there, so I just kind of kept my eyes open a little bit and looked up every once in awhile. I kept falling asleep but at some point I heard the males who

136

went out to hunt come back and I saw they were carrying a dead moose, or at least a moose in several pieces, each male carrying about one fourth of it. At least I think it was a moose, its head was gone."

"I fell asleep at some point, but I'm sure they were still going at it when I finally passed out. When I woke up it was morning and next to my bed was a fresh plate of fish cooked with some greens, I didn't know what they were but it was delicious. The little ones as soon as they saw I was up were all over me, tickling me and playing with my hair. Their mothers called them not to bother me, but I let them know it was all right. We seemed to be able to speak to each other without saying anything. If I said something, they understood me and when they motioned or grunted at me, I understood them. They motioned for me to follow them, and they took me inside the cave to what must have been a mineral water spring, except the water was warm. I know there are some geothermal springs in the area, and this had to be one of them. There were candles lit and furs laid out I was sure for my benefit."

"While I bathed only one of the other females was in there with me, and she seemed sad. She looked very young and had spots like a leopard, a very beautiful coat. She even had long hair like a girl, and she had full lips and big eyes. She kind of reminded me of those cartoon girls, 'Josie and the Pussycats' the way her hips were so human, she looked like a girl in a snug fitting leopard outfit. After wrapping up in furs I asked her what was wrong and she took my hand and led me to another part of the cave. She brought one of the candles for me to see, I was pretty sure they didn't need them."

"On every inch of cave walls there were paintings, but they didn't look like caveman paintings, they were more like a graphic novel you'd buy at a bookstore, full of color and detail. No words, just pictures, but very artistic, as if done by a professional. She pointed at one area of the wall that showed a picture of her with what looked like her with her mate and a small child. They looked happy together but there was another drawing of a white man they seemed to have found in the woods bleeding. I couldn't tell if it was from a hunting accident or an animal attack, but they seemed to be in a cabin or hunting blind. The next picture showed the same man playing with the little one, and what I assumed to be the male tending the man's wounds. The one after that showed them all together, as if they painted a portrait to celebrate the man's recovery, and they all looked happy."

"Then she took my hand and pointed a few paintings down, and it showed the same man with a gun and the male and the little one in a cage, the male was raging mad. There were some other white men in the painting who weren't there before. The next painting showed what had to be a fierce battle, there were several white men and several male Bigfoot creatures. Then the last painting showed all of them dead, and her mate and child being carried away by the other creatures, but they were carried as if to a funeral. Then there was a picture of just her, I guessed to signify her new status as an available mate, but the same sadness I saw in her eyes was in the painting."

"Then she walked me to another part of the cave where there was a painting of another male, and he looked to be fighting a group of animals. There was blood all over and it looked like what I was sure were wolves. The next portrait showed the creatures back in the cave tending to their wounds, but there was someone lying on the floor who was being looked after. I looked closer and realized that the person on the floor was me. They hadn't just rescued me, they had to fight the wolves to save me and it looked as though some of them were badly injured. The next painting was me looking all better, but still asleep. Then there was a painting of me running away from the cave holding a torch. That was the last painting. Then the female pointed at the painting of me running away, and pointed back to the painting of the man they had saved before and the cages her mate and young one had been put in. They had saved this man's life and he turned on them and kidnapped them to get rich or expose them or whatever, but her young one was killed as well as her mate."

"She was asking me if I was going to betray them as well. Is that what I'm doing now, or am I saving them by telling you? If I don't tell the truth or the police think I'm lying if I tell a different story about what happened to me, they're going to send up a search party to look for some psycho teenage girl kidnapper and they're going to find my friends. I had to tell you because I need your help. I can't tell the truth and if I lie they'll know and go looking up there. Can you help me?"

CHAPTER FOURTEEN

Brenda took a huge breath and had been frozen in one spot for so long her legs were cramping, so she had to move them. Emily looked to be almost in tears after her story, which Brenda couldn't tell if she was completely psychotic, a brilliant con artist, a traumatized kidnap victim, or telling what would amount to the greatest story of her career. As she sat there wondering exactly what to say there was a knock and Brian stuck his head in. Brenda was never so thankful to be interrupted.

"Hey I gotta grab the camera, one of the rescue guys is here and I want to get a statement. Don't worry Bren, I know what to do." It was a gamble, knowing that Emily might want to say hi or thank one of the guys who helped to find her, but luckily she sat there without saying anything. Just as Brian put his hand on the camera, the camera made a CLICK WHIRRRRR sound that Brenda knew well, but Emily wouldn't. Had Brian walked in ten seconds later, Emily would have known the camera was on the whole time.

"So everything good in here?" Brenda nodded, her mouth still open. Brian had never seen her so speechless, so he just asked, "You guys want anything else when I come back? More coffee, something to eat?" Brenda and Emily both shook their heads, and Brian was out the door. Brian knew he had gotten that one right and gotten every bit of what Emily was saying, or as much as he could, and checked his watch to come in right at the two hour mark and gotten the camera right as it clicked off. It was a nail biter, hoping that the camera had a two-hour tape in it and trying to time it so he came in at the end of the tape, but he made it just in time. He knew his reward would come later that night in the hotel room. Maybe Emily would join them.

Back in the room, Emily was looking at Brenda waiting for her to say something. Brenda, who was NEVER at a loss for words, just shook her head and decided since she had gotten away with the interview this far on tape, that from now on, honesty was the best policy and if the girl turned out to be a time waster, at least she had a great story on tape, even if she couldn't use it.

"I want to help you, of course. But what you're asking me to do is…. well, what IS it you're asking me to do? Do you want me to help you make up some cover story about how some Native Canadian kidnapped you and took you to his cabin and held you hostage and you fell in love with him? The statement I got from the police before I met you was that you didn't want to be brought in, and you were crying for the police to leave them alone. If what you're telling me is true, I can see why you would want them to be left in peace, but if you're covering for someone else and trying to get me to play a part in that, there's no fucking way. Now I'm a reporter. Do you know what that means?"

Emily shook her head in a girlish way, like no matter what Brenda said, she should be able to do what she wanted.

"It means that I have an obligation to let the people of the world know what is going on in an unbiased and objective fashion, something that is dying out. Major corporations are buying all of the news agencies, and even social media like Twitter and YouTube are controlled by corporate entities. There are PLENTY of people being blacklisted on the Internet, not just talked badly about, but also having their whole Internet presence erased. If they try to put up a story, and the search engine finds words leading to a city, a person, or a subject THEY don't want talked about, it'll be erased before it even gets uploaded. I've got a jump on that. I've got an advantage, and it keeps me IN THE KNOWLEDGE of what is really going on, and I'm allowed to fly from city to city all over the world just to let people know what is happening. If all of this is true, it is my DUTY to let people know. But I can see that it would also be the end of these 'things', if they do, in fact, exist."

"So here's what's going to happen. You're going to tell me the rest of the story and tell me why you didn't want to come home. Then I'LL decide if it's worth putting on the news. Having your pretty little face come home is a good story. Catching the guys who may have taken you is an even better story, but if there were 'bigfoot' creatures living up in the Canadian wilderness and you knew where they were, that would be the biggest story of the DECADE. And those people who control the media? The 'THEY' who decide what the public gets to hear and doesn't? Well darling, ONE of 'they' is the guy who signs my check every week, and this is one of those stories that wouldn't get blacklisted, so it would be front-page news WORLD WIDE. Both of us would become HUGE celebrities, and be SURE that's something you would REALLY want BEFORE YOU WISH FOR IT. Phillip Seymour Hoffman, the actor, just died of a heroin overdose, and I would be covering THAT story, OR the Japan/Chinese peace talks, so YOU had

BETTER figure out how you want this story to end, because let me tell you darling, those paintings on the cave? They're still being drawn, and you're the star of this one, and it is NOT over yet. So I can bring him one of two stories. Which one it is, at this point, is up to you."

Emily looked hurt. She was hoping for a different response, one of reassurance and compassion, not to be told she was in hot water over this. She thought about it for a minute. She wondered if telling this woman was the right thing to do. She was so used to guys doing whatever they told her to do, begging for her pussy that she figured the rest of the world bent over for pretty girls too. She seemed to consider for a minute how insane her story sounded, but she had come this far and was going to have to convince this woman to see things her way, and the only way to do that was to be believed. Emily didn't think that she would believe her own story either, but she didn't stop to think about his before she started telling it to Brenda.

"All right. I'll tell you the rest, but the decision is yours, not mine. It is a pretty fantastic thing to ask someone to believe, and all I can do is tell you what happened, so where the story ends up is up to YOU, not me."

Brenda knew she was right. She was really hoping that Emily was going to stop all this nonsense about attacking wolf packs and graphic novel writing ape-men, especially ones that looked like furry stuffed animals and not the hulking beasts that were prevalent in the tales of drunken Canadian gold prospectors and isolated hunters.

"Why have I always heard of these creatures being giant Neanderthal looking beasts, walking bears or upright gorillas? Why are yours different?"

"Well, that's a good question, but think about it like this. A dog comes and barks and bites at a man. That same dog comes up to a lady and jumps in her lap, licks her face, and begs for treats and pets. Ask her to describe the animal and she'll tell you it's a lovely creature, soft and warm with a beautiful coat. Ask a man the same question and he'll tell you it was a ferocious beast, teeth three inches long and razor sharp, with a wild look in its eye and coarse, matted fur. Even the early explorers of Africa and Australia describe fearsome looking creatures that have never been seen again, leopard men, mermaids, werewolves, sea monsters..."

"Bigfoot", Brenda interrupted, and Emily looked down. She was getting the idea Brenda thought she was wasting her time, and she was right. Brenda had been so caught up in wanting to believe this hot vixen, especially after they shared such a wonderful day together, that she started to think maybe this girl was playing her. Brenda looked at Emily with a stern look that said, "I'm waiting", and Emily shifted uncomfortably in her seat.

CHAPTER FIFTEEN

"I knew that these creatures were taking a risk by allowing me to see everything about them, where they lived, how they lived, and I wondered how long ago there were larger tribes of them, were they here when Columbus landed? Had they been friends with the natives? Or had they always been isolated and few in number? There are many kinds of animals that are few in number and scattered widely, few and far between, even I've read enough to know that it's possible. But many creatures are being discovered even today that are large, I read a certain gazelle was discovered in Vietnam only a few years ago, and they were undiscovered up until now"

"But the gazelle wasn't a man like walking creature with giant feet, nor has it been written about for centuries in books and tales"

"But these things HAVE, don't you see? They've been written about, photographed, sighted, and I know that the natives and locals know about them, but just don't want their land overrun with, well, reporters. They were so gentle. There was no aggression in them unless attacked, and then it seemed that they carried away their dead. Even Magellan described South American people with tails, and THAT was only a few hundred years ago."

Brenda was impressed with Emily's knowledge. She was right. Magellan HAD described people who lived in snow without clothing, and people with small tails that lived in South America. In fact, there have been dozens of creatures described by explorers and sailors that weren't seen again for sometimes hundreds of years. Brenda remembered a story she declined about a fisherman who had apparently seen a mermaid, but she knew there was no evidence and she rarely took stories on word of mouth. There were too many people who just wanted attention or had other reasons for lying to journalists, and one of them was being kidnapped and then falling for the person who kidnapped you, or falling for a refugee from the law and needing an excuse to be absent for a month. Emily was news simply because she was found alive, and a pretty face is always newsworthy. Emily was all the evidence Brenda needed to take the story, but to go further, she needed more than a wild story about Bigfoot. "All right, I'm sorry I interrupted you. Please continue."

"I wanted to reassure them that I wasn't going to betray them. I tried to watch what the women were doing when there was enough light, and tried to imitate them. Soon I was skinning small animals and cutting up strips of meat from raccoons and deer that we placed on the bicycle wheel to cook. They took great pleasure in this, mostly because I was so terrible at it, but they laughed good-naturedly at my attempts to imitate them and helped when they could. We all ate together around a fire, and I played with the young ones who couldn't get enough of me. The older females actually seemed to be relieved of the obligation to care for them all day, and I thoroughly enjoyed them, so I was given the honor and prestigious position of babysitter and caretaker of the young during the day."

"The only one who never seemed to communicate with me was the snow white female. I think she was used to being the center of attention and it felt like I was taking their minds off of her. There were older females who seemed to hold higher rank, they definitely had a pecking order, but she seemed to be most popular with the males. They paid special attention to her and when they came back from hunting she was given small gifts, like a mirror one time, even a ball of tinfoil, anything shiny, even if it might have been worthless to you and me. I tried to show her I wasn't a threat, but the males seemed to want to take an interest in me, and I think she was jealous of that. That's the curse of being a pretty girl, as I'm sure you know."

Brenda knew EXACTLY what Emily was talking about. Brenda had been the pretty girl her whole life, and anyone who thinks that life is easy for pretty girls is dead wrong. Other girls HATE you because men pay attention to you, sometimes their boyfriends, sometimes their husbands. Men despise you for refusing their advances and then spread rumors about you, telling everyone you're a slut, or they fucked you when you wouldn't give them the time of day. Brenda had to fight for everything she had her whole life, and even still people told everyone she had things 'given' to her just because she was pretty. It was nice to get attention, but many times that attention was unwanted, and sometimes people didn't take no for an answer. She thought about older men who tried to take advantage of her when she was still a child, and remembered often wishing she was fat and ugly so that no one would pay so much attention to her.

"I began to feel at home with them. I felt honored they trusted me with their children, but I still felt like a visitor who may have overstayed her welcome. I wanted to show them that I was one of them, and that I wanted to stay. I have never felt so loved by any group of people, even my own family. There was only one way I could think of to show them that I was one of them."

"That night as usual, after the food was all eaten and the children put to bed, we all drank that stuff that made you feel so good. I had a few extra glasses because I was getting up the courage to try my plan and see if it worked. After a little while everyone began to separate into couples, and the females had this little ritual when they were ready to mate. They rolled around in the fur making purring noises, and moved into a submissive position, some on their backs, some on their knees doggy style, but almost all of them did it. I could tell some of them weren't even into it but they did it to satisfy their mates, who were happy to oblige."

"I began rolling around in my furs, making, or trying to make, the same purring noises. I felt a little silly at first, but it kind of comes naturally. The only difference was that everyone already had a mate, and I was in bed alone. They always switched partners during the night anyway, so I was thinking one of them might come over to me. Anyway after a few minutes of doing this I found my natural rhythm and I found myself really turned on. The others were already going at it, and it was like watching a giant orgy, only everyone had fur. Their coats were all soft and glowing from having just been groomed as part of their nightly ritual, and I found myself wishing I had a coat like that. Anyway, I kept listening to them fuck, and that and rolling around and touching myself got me really wet. I decided to just get myself off since no one was paying any attention to me."

"I lay on my back and spread my legs. It was actually a real turn on, being in a crowd and showing off my pussy. I imagined everyone was looking at me and wanting to fuck me like mad. This got me even hotter, and I started playing with myself. I kept running my fingers all up and down my pussy, feeling my clit throbbing and listening to the wild animals fuck each other. It started to make me crazy. I got up on all fours and stuck my fingers in myself, fingering my pussy and licking the juice off of my fingers. I had never been so turned on and wanted to get fucked SO bad, but all I could do was keep fingering myself and trying to make myself come."

"Just then one of the males climbed behind me and grabbed my ass. He pulled at my ass and spread it apart like you want a man to, just to come and fuck me HARD. He seemed to pick up on that, and even I could smell how wet I was. The next thing I knew his dick was pushing up against me, asking me if I wanted it. He was hard as a rock and I had to turn around and see what I was dealing with, and Brenda, once that furry foreskin was off his cock looked the same as a humans but it was HUGE! It was at LEAST ten inches long and three inches around! I was so insane I just grabbed it and shoved his cock to the back of my throat, sucking him off for all I was worth. He was looking down at me, and in the darkness he looked like a guy wearing a fur coat, only with a huge dick and a hot blonde going down on him...He grabbed me with ONE HAND and LIFTED me up so I was on my knees in front of him! I've never had anyone pick me up so easily, it was SO much fun! It felt like he could throw me around the bed like a toy! He spread my legs and shoved his cock inside me, and GOD did if feel GOOD! He started pounding away at me, and I was so juiced up that he hardly had to push, only because I was so tight! He was just using me for a little fucktoy, and I gotta say it was the best fuck I've EVER had! When a wild animal takes you, you KNOW it's a wild animal! I was almost being lifted off the bed by his cock, sometimes only my hands or elbows were on the bed, and my ass was lifted up in the air with my pussy getting punished ferociously...."

"The next thing I knew, I was on my back, and my fingers were running through his coat. I know it felt good for him because I see them grooming every day, so it had to feel as good as it does to us...Looking at his face, he was just beautiful...Streaked blonde hair, almost like a surfer's with huge shoulder muscles, and blue eyes...did I mention they all had different colored eyes? Well his were blue, and he looked at me with such lust, I was surprised they hadn't gotten on me before this! He started going faster and faster, and I could feel him getting ready to pop.... I pulled my legs up by my ears, and he put his hands under my knees and FUCKED me so hard I thought I was going to pass out! His foreskin, which was all fur, was rubbing right on my clit, and it was heaven.... I'm going to have to have someone make vibrators with fur clit stimulators, because once that started to rub me, I started coming right there. My moaning and crying must have driven him over the edge, because he started shoving it in me so hard I could feel the bottom of my ribcage getting hit but I LOVED it! He shot his load inside me with a giant grunt, and rolled off me once he was done with me."

"I wanted to grab him and lay with him, or get him to at least fuck me again, but there was another one ready to start! This one was darker with grey stripes. I was getting to be able to tell them all apart, but this one didn't even bother with formalities like the first one did. This one just got on top of me and used my pussy to get off in about three minutes, but when all of their cocks are so fucking big, each one is like something you'd pay for, but I was getting it for free! It turned into an all night gang bang, each one of them grabbing me and throwing me however they wanted, pounding me until early morning. I could tell they had ALL wanted to fuck me from the first night. They were such gentle creatures though, you know with guys like that you gotta make the first move."

"The next night I woke up feeling guilty, like everyone does after the first time they try something new. I wondered if I was going to go to hell, if this was an abomination, or I was some kind of carnival freak or something you'd see in one of those bestiality movies on the Internet. Should I be disgusted with myself or proud? I didn't think about it too long, because from that point on, I was one of the family. Every day I took care of the little ones, bathing and playing with them while the other women worked and the men slept, and every night after the hunt we ate together and drank until we were tipsy and then the party began. It was a constant giant orgy, and all of the females got to take turns being the star. I helped them groom their coats, and they brought me fresh food and clean pelts to sleep on."

"Days turned into weeks and I figured by then I had been there at least twenty days. I wasn't sure what day it was, because I didn't know how long I was delirious with fever the second time they saved me, but I couldn't have been off by more than a few days, and honestly, I didn't care. For the first time in my life I didn't give a shit about what time it was or what day it was. When we were hungry, we ate. When we were sleepy, we slept, and when we were horny, which was every night, we fucked. My hair and nails were growing out. I usually feel disgusting if I don't shave my legs every three or four days, but I was growing hair all over and I didn't mind at all. In fact, I was still wishing that I could grow a coat like theirs, but no matter how long I didn't shave my legs I'd never look like them."

"There was something else special. Every night, the last Bigfoot to fuck me was always one who seemed to be the oldest of the adolescents; I guess he was just in early adulthood. He was light brown with blue black spots and streaks, but the skin under the coat was lighter, like almost sand colored. He wanted to be the last one every night so he could lay with me, and every morning I woke up in his arms, held tight in a giant blanket of warm fur. It was like falling in love, but you got the added pleasure of a whole roomful of lovers and no jealousy. He wasn't possessive or temperamental, but at night when he came back from the hunt he always had something for me like a honeycomb, which was a nightmare for them to carry because the honey would get their fur all sticky and had to be cleaned out, which I think he loved having me do and that's why he brought them for me. It was SO sweet and charming, like when Elvis had that kid kick him in the shins so he had an excuse to see that nurse he had a crush on in that movie... He even brought me a necklace that was made with shells and beads. They were very adept at using tools, and I was never surprised at how ingenious

152

they were. I wouldn't at all have been surprised if I walked into one of the rooms and seen one of them flipping channels with a remote."

"I took his presents and attention as a sign of love, and tried to give him something special every day too. I'd make sure he had something extra to eat that he liked, or I'd be the one to groom him at the end of the day. You know there's something in us that we've lost living in cities and being addicted to computers and televisions. Everything in that cave I did came so second nature to me, but it was everything I LOVED doing. Paying attention to or having attention paid to me by someone I cared about or playing with cute fuzzy kids, having my hair and body stroked and scratched at least an hour every night, bathing and washing was even a pleasure, and though I didn't smell the same, after eating so much natural food for a few weeks I lost what I thought was body odor, but it's just all of the chemicals and preservatives we eat coming out of us. Our bodies process the food, but rejects the chemicals, and that's what smells on us, so we use more chemicals to cover it up."

"I never thought I could be so happy. I wanted to stay there forever, and thought I was welcome to. I certainly felt like I was welcome, and every day was something I was thankful for. There was no ownership of anything. If you wanted something, you used it, if someone else needed it, they waited until you were finished, and if it broke, they found the person or whatever you'd call them, they were people to me, who was the best at making it, and you should see the pride in their faces as they made what was needed. They were so proud to be the best at making something, they all put a tremendous amount of pride into anything they did, whether it was a weapon to hunt with, or a knife to skin animals with, even combs were prized for their usefulness and beauty. I never wanted it to end. But much too soon, the walls came crashing down."

CHAPTER SIXTEEN

Brenda was spellbound once again. What she thought was a clever story had her wrapped up and speechless, thinking she was going to go crazy trying to decide if this was all real or not. She wanted it to be real more than anything in her life, but that's how con artists get you. She was old enough to know that. A really good con gets you to WANT to believe the story you get suckered into, and the next thing you know, you're INSISTING that person take all of your money, your trust, or whatever. Brenda KNEW she couldn't be taken in by a bullshitter, but what if it was real? She could have the greatest story of the century here, and if she blew it off without investigating it further she could lose it to someone else. But what was worse? Feeling like she was being suckered, or getting the time and resources from the newspaper to go up there and find nothing and be made into a fool? Or would it be worse if it was all true, and she did nothing? Worse yet, what if it was true, and she DID investigate it, only to have some beautiful, peaceful civilization of mans closest relative on the planet suddenly lose their homes, have their family torn apart, and live in some concentration camps? Even if it was a lab or a zoo with trees and shit, she knew it would be a concentration camp for them. If they were real, and she did that to them, she would never forgive herself. Brenda had seen enough of what war does to people, what genocide does, and she would be directly responsible for it. Her head swam as she thought about all of this, but Emily wasn't finished yet.

"One night the males all came back from the hunt. They had no prey with them, but they were very excited. They went into the back room and I could hear all kinds of jabbering and movement, and I knew there was trouble, but I didn't know what it was. Then I heard the white coated female. Her voice was very beautiful, almost like a mewing, but with all vowels, very pretty and high pitched. I was getting better at understanding them and even understood a few basic verbal gestures but this was beyond my comprehension. After what seemed like an hour of them discussing whatever it was, they all came back and lay in bed. There was no party, no drink to make us feel good, and no sex. Something was very, VERY wrong. The only thing that made me stop fretting was that my mate, well, I guess at this point you could call him that, came to lay down with me. He made me feel so safe, like nothing could hurt me or get to me if I was with him. I was soon to find out how wrong I was."

"The next morning the males left before sunup. They were looking for something, at least that's the impression I got. One of the females told me the bath was ready, and I went into the part of the cave where the bath was. It also was the part of the cave that had my story on it, and there were a few more paintings, so stopped to look. There was a new painting of me ill with fever, then another of me all better and playing with the little ones, which made me smile. The next painting showed me in bed with my mate, and I was sure he drew it. That meant more to me than any present I had been given by anyone else in the world. We looked so beautiful together. He truly looked happy. Then I stood in shock at what I saw."

"There was a painting that wasn't of me, but it was my storyline. It was a crudely painted picture of a black and white box with something red on top. I didn't know what it was at first, but then I realized it was a police car. They were searching for me, and they had gotten as close as the hunting grounds. They had to be within fifteen to twenty miles. You might think that's a long way, and in the wilderness it is. A twenty mile radius is a forty mile diameter, and if you do the math, that's a LOT of square mileage to cover. I could see dogs in the picture, though, and the dogs would find my scent, and if not mine, the scent of one of my family. I had led the police right to their home, and they were going to keep looking for me. They knew I hadn't drowned; I had disappeared from a tent in the middle of the night. My boyfriend was going to tell them that I was just gone, and there were probably tracks by the campsite. They weren't thinking I had drowned. They thought I was still alive, and they were getting close."

"I started to cry. I didn't want to leave. I bawled the whole time I was in the spring, trying to make myself feel better, but I just felt worse. If I stayed here, they would all be in danger. If I left, I would be leaving the best thing in my life EVER behind. I loved them. I truly did. I decided I would wait to see what they would want to do. Maybe they had a summer cave we could escape to, you know, like in "Dances With Wolves", or some other way to get out of this. They had survived for so long by being evasive, why couldn't they think of something now?"

"I got out of my bath, still sobbing to see the white coated female standing in front of me. She gave me some furs to dry off with, which I thought was a sign that we were on the same side, but I was wrong. After I was dry, she handed me my clothes that I had been brought here in. It was my flannel, my hiking shorts, socks, boots, even my underwear had all been washed, and my guess was to take out the scent so the dogs wouldn't find me. Next to that was the survival bag she had given me the first time I left. She was telling me to go, and giving me an excuse as well. If I was smart, I could tell them I had a lighter, and a few essentials and was able to hunt and fish or at least collect nuts and berries the last few weeks to stay alive. When I saw all of these things together I burst into tears again."

"I knew what I had to do. If I stayed, they would have caught up with me and we would have been separated anyway, but my friends would have been put into some zoo or been dissected, no matter what it would have been hell for them. They hadn't survived this long being stupid, but then again, there weren't that many of them. I spent what I knew would be my last day playing with the little ones who wouldn't understand what was going on, but there were lots of hugs for them and playing and tickling and they made me smile but every time I looked at them and knew I wouldn't see them again I cried. They held me as if they knew something was wrong, and I held them tight. I was scared."

"When the men came back that evening, they seemed to have a plan together. They had drawn out a map, and for the first time I could see where I was. They had actually taken me south from the peninsula, and that's why I couldn't find the bay last time I left. They were going to take me west, leading the search away from the cave. It would lead the search party in the exact opposite direction from where they were, so they would be safe. For the rest of the night I hugged and groomed each one of them, except for the white-coated female, who seemed to have an air about her like time was running short. She never wanted me there in the first place, and now she was afraid I was staying too long and it was dangerous for them. I didn't want to leave, and cried and told them all that I loved them. They howled and sang in a low voice, like when a dog is lonely for its master. I knew they loved me too, and they were going to miss me. It was a very difficult day for us, and we ate together for the last time."

CHAPTER SEVENTEEN

"After we had eaten and everyone was gathering themselves for what I assumed would be my exodus, one by one the young ones started coming up to me. One of them pulled me by the arm and showed me a painting he had done of me. It was something like a child would have done; only he put it over his own bed. I knew he wanted to see me every night before he went to bed and it made me start to cry. The other young ones all wanted to play with me, but the elder females pulled them down. They all looked like they were crying. I had never seen one of them cry, but they expressed the emotion of sadness just the same. One of the little girls showed me a doll she had made, and it had locks of blonde hair and was definitely human. It was a little doll of me, so I took a sharp piece of glass and cut off a length of my hair so she could put it on the doll. All of the young ones reached out for a piece of my hair so I gave a little to each of them."

"Then the adult females came up to me one at a time to say goodbye. They hugged me and stroked my hair, some smiling and wishing me luck in their own way and some just looking sad and forlorn. I could tell that they had all made gifts for me, but it seemed to be understood that if I showed up with a bunch of tools and toys looking like they had been made by a stone age tribe of Indians, there would be too much speculation about what had really happened to me. I understood this even though we couldn't speak. They're remarkably intelligent, you know."

"After that it was totally dark out, and the males motioned to me it was time to go. The little ones held my hand all the way out of the cave, and they all walked with me to the end of the glade at the bottom or the ridge their cave was in. It was a very emotional moment for all of us. I bawled like I was going to my execution, which is what it felt like more than being led to the police who would bring me home. At the end of the glade there were a group of trees and beyond that was the forest. I turned around to see them all one last time, and cried very hard. Some of the young were pulling away from their mothers, wanting to come with me, but they were held fast. They made a deep low wailing, the saddest noise I had ever heard them make. It wasn't like a howl or a dog crying, more like a giant jungle cat when it is in pain. I think all creatures share that instinct that when they suffer they cry. I was totally beside myself."

"There were four males that were with me, and one of them was my mate. The others had been the ones who rescued me, one of them had been the one who brought me back the second time and he was the first one to, initiate me I guess you would call it, to their nightly ritual. After about an hour of walking I was thankful they had kept my hiking boots and socks. After another hour, the big one pointed to my khaki shorts and motioned for me to take them off. I thought at first he wanted to fuck me one last time, and I was totally confused but didn't want to say no. When I took them off, he grabbed them out of my hands and placed them on the end of a long stick that I thought was a spear. He then ran them along the ground after us. We had been walking for about two hours at a pretty good clip, and my mate had even carried me for about forty-five minutes through some thickets and overgrowth. As I said, they can see really well in the dark and it was easier to carry me to keep moving fast. I'd say we were at least fifteen miles away from their cave."

"We kept walking all night, and every time I got cold my mate picked me up and I wrapped my legs around his waist. He was so warm and carried me like I was nothing. I hadn't felt like that since my dad carried me when I was a little girl, just completely trusting and loving. Now here was the man I loved, or the beast anyway, carrying me like I was a little girl again. I hung my head in his shoulder and cried."

"The next morning we were still walking, and I was so tired, but I don't think they wanted to let me go until I was near civilization. I think the plan was to go near a town where I could call someone or at least let the police there know who I was and they would call off the search, but that's not what happened. They heard it long before I did, or caught the scent, but suddenly they started running. My mate just picked me up like a toy and started running through the forest and then I heard it. I could hear dogs barking in the distance, dogs that are on to a scent. Hunters move slow with dogs, but once the dogs have a scent, they'll let them go and some dogs can catch the prey and others will tree it, and others will just keep following it, howling to let their masters know that this was where whatever it was they were looking for is located."

"As they ran still carrying me, I could hear the dogs getting closer and closer. Next thing I knew, I could hear a helicopter in the area. I guess they radioed in that the dogs had a scent. They were running at full speed now, trying to use paths where their footsteps wouldn't be seen. They were very conscious of that the whole time. As the helicopter and the dogs got closer and closer, I started to panic. What was going to happen when they found us? Would they already know about these creatures and just let them go, thanking them for saving me, or would they start shooting at them, trying to mount one of their heads on the wall?"

"The chopper was almost right on top of us. The dogs were less than a few hundred yards away, and I thought they were going to have to fight their way out of this. I never got to find out because the next thing I knew I was on the ground HARD, and at first I thought I had slipped out of my mate's hands. But the truth was he dropped me right where I was and took off running in the other direction. I couldn't believe it. No goodbye, no hug, nothing from him or the other males. They just dropped me and ran. I was furious. I started screaming after him, but I didn't even know if he HAD a name, so what was I going to say? I just screamed and screamed as the helicopter spotted me and came into the clearing I was near to land."

"I had NEVER in my thoughts imagined that he would just drop me and run at full pace away from me without even saying goodbye. The larger one took off with my shorts on the end of the stick, so I was sitting there in just a shirt and boots, screaming and crying while these dogs started jumping and slobbering all over me and the rescue workers got out of the chopper. I was screaming after my lover, knowing I would never see him again, but it was such a horrible injustice to be just dropped like that, I didn't get to tell him goodbye. I didn't get to tell him

I loved him. As I shouted after him, wanting to just even see him for a second over the ridge looking back to see if I was okay or ANYTHING, the rescue workers were trying to get me to hold still and get me in the chopper. I fought them so hard, I just wanted to say goodbye. I wanted to know he was safe and the dogs weren't going to go after them. I wanted some form of knowledge that he was safe and would be waiting for me to return some day, but he was just gone. And that's all there is."

CHAPTER EIGHTEEN

Brenda sat there with her mouth open again trying to decide what to say. She was furious she missed getting this last part on camera, but there was nothing that could be done about that. Even if Emily told the exact same story again, there's something to a first time telling, something about it being in confidence that ties it in an aura of tension and mystery she could never recapture. She wished more than ANYTHING Brian would walk in right then with a few cups of coffee or an urgent message to call the office. Brenda had never HEARD such a story in her entire news career, and wasn't sure what to make of it. She could either believe it or not believe it, and if she believed it she could either help Emily cover it up, or she could pursue the holy grail of investigative reporting. If she chose NOT to believe it, she had to decide whether to air the footage she had and portray Emily as a crazy but very sexy kidnap victim (she was going to look great on air either way), or go ahead and shoot an all new interview and let Emily tell a new story of survival on her own in the forest of North Canada.

"What, ummm, and then I guess the police questioned you after they brought you in? What did you tell them?"

"I told them that yes, someone had helped me but no, they hadn't kidnapped me and they would much rather be left alone. They told me many times a kidnap victim was so scared of her abductor that she protected him just so that he wouldn't come after her or her family if she talked, and that's what they thought was happening. I can tell you still might think that too."

Brenda closed her eyes for a second. She wasn't a praying woman, but she was saying to herself, ".... I MUST make the right decision here". She opened her eyes and looked at Emily, who seemed to be happy to have told someone, and she even looked a little confident that Brenda might take her side. She was hopeful of this anyway. She tossed it around in her head for a minute, and then tried a new play.

"Emily, tell you what. Let's try this. You let me interview you ON TAPE, and you say what you want. I've only got another few hours here then I've got to either fly you to Los Angeles or go cover another story. I've got to send something in to my editor. Let me turn the camera on you. You say what YOU want, and we'll see what he says. But first of all, is there any proof, ANY proof at all what you say is true? Did you have your smartphone with you? Did you take any pictures? That's the only thing I could think of that would qualify, unless we all went back to the cave together, and I don't have the time nor do I have the resources for an offline shoot like that, so before I do what you want, I need for you to PROVE to me that what you're saying is real. You do that, and you can call your own shots. Otherwise. It's by the book."

Emily wasn't expecting this. Brenda was turning out to be a very tough and very smart girl. She was hoping to just be believed, and then she could concoct a story with Brenda's help that would make everyone happy and not go looking around up there for kidnappers or Bigfoot. She had no idea how to move forward now. There was only one thing she could do.

"Tell you what. Give me an interview and I'll go on tape saying that Canadian Aborigines helped me. You fly back to Los Angeles and after the heat has died down, I'll go back there with a video camera and I'll get you your proof, BUT that proof is only for YOU as payment for helping me, NOT to expose them to the world. Does that sound like a fair deal?"

"NO IT DOES NOT. SO you're asking me to help you out NOW, and in exchange, you'll do me a favor LATER. Well, that's called a sucker play, and I'm not falling for it. If you want me to convince the police NOT to go looking around up there, and to help you come up with a story that will convince them as well as the rest of the world, I need you to come up with something NOW. I'm not risking my career, lying to the world about what happened to you. If the truth, WHATEVER that is came out, I'd lose my journalistic credibility. I'll tell you again. If you can come up with the proof that will convince me that what you've told me is true, I'll do whatever you want to help you, but if you want me to help you just on your word alone, I'm sorry but I can't do that."

"And you know what, YOU'VE gotten ME in a very tricky spot ALSO. What am I supposed to do at this point? I can't risk putting you on camera, sure I could interview you, but the choice to air you isn't mine, it's the choice of my employers. You're so pretty you could whistle Dixie out of your asshole and no one would care, they just want to see a pretty girl on television, but to me what you say DOES matter. Every broadcast I do, every story I present to the world I'm putting my reputation on the line. If this thing falls apart I'm fucking myself badly and for what? For you? Honey, you're sweet and hey, it was fun, but don't think I'm going to put THAT kind of trust in you and don't be offended, it's just reality."

"I'm going to get Brian in here. We're going to start rolling in about fifteen minutes so start doing your makeup and hair, I'll give you a quick touchup before we go on. You can say whatever you want, I can't force you either way, but if it sounds like shit and you're not convincing, don't expect me to support you and say, "Oh, honey you poor thing! Whatever did you do next?" I'm a journalist, so I'm expected to ask tough questions, so be ready to answer them. And remember, I'll go as easy on you as you make it easy for me, so if you can be as convincing with your story as you just were with your last one, you should be fine no matter WHAT you say."

"But the story I just told you was the TRUTH! How is anything going to sound more convincing than the truth?"

"I don't know doll, but you'd better think of something quick. BRIAN! Hey, can you put that sweater I brought for you on? Your tits looked great in that!"

Emily smiled an unconvincing smile and puttered about the room getting dressed and made up. Brian came in the room with hot coffee for the girls and the camera all ready to go. He plugged everything in, set up the chairs and checked the light levels, put up "QUIET- LIVE BROADCAST IN PROGRESS" signs in the hallways, and made suggestions to the girls about where to look and place their hands, what the camera was going to show, and so on. He was very professional, and when he snapped into action, he was worth every penny the news agency paid him. He sat the girls down in their seats, reminded them that this was a tape, not a live broadcast, so they could edit out any misspoken words or phrases, so if there was a mistake, just to start over. He gave them the all clear, and counted down in 3...2...1...and pointed at Brenda.

CHAPTER NINETEEN

"This is Brenda Nova, coming to you from Quebec, Canada where Emily Wrennington has just been rescued after surviving for almost four weeks in the Canadian wilderness. How are you feeling, Emily?"

"Oh, I feel great, thanks."

"You were found by rescue workers yesterday after the search for you had just about been called off according to reports by local authorities. What were the circumstances surrounding your disappearance and led to you being missing for almost an entire month?"

"Well, I was injured by a nasty fall and I was bleeding. That night, a pack of wolves who I guess could smell the blood and knew by our campfire that there was food in our campsite, only they thought the food was me" and laughed a very nervous laugh, hoping Brenda would play along but she didn't, just nodding her head and not even cracking a smile.

"There was a tribe of local native Canadians nearby, or I guess there was a reservation, or just enough of them lived close by to call it a community. Some of them were out at night and heard the wolves, or heard, us, because I was really scared and we had been drinking, so ......I............" At this point Emily stopped and stuttered, looking to Brenda for help, but there was none coming. Emily just went on as best she could.

"I think I was blacked out, all I remember was being carried upside down, and the next thing I new I was in a cabin with a twisted ankle, unable to walk."

"But why were you missing? Wouldn't they just call or let someone know that you had been found?"

Emily glared at Brenda. "You fucking bitch" was all she could think. She had to come up with something, so she just took a deep breath, and went on.

"I asked them not to tell anyone where I was. I had been fighting with an ex boyfriend, and I was afraid he was going to hurt the guy I was dating at the time. He was that kind of a guy. Yeah, if he knew where I was, he'd come looking for me, so I asked them not to tell anybody. Then I got a fever, a really bad one, and was sick for the next few weeks."

"And no one thought to bring you to a hospital? You were in bed for three or four weeks, somebody who's that sick I would hope that they at least tried to provide some sort of medical service for you."

DAMN she was tough. The one thing that was happening though, was that Brenda was ACUTELY aware of the fact that she was asking for details, details that the person who told her a story of being abducted by bigfoot would be able to make up on the spot if they were that clever and that good of a liar. If Emily stumbled, and she was, then Brenda was going to give her story more credibility. In fact, Emily was so bad at making up this story about being rescued by native Canadian Indians that Brenda thought there was NO WAY she could have made up the other story. The simple fact was that some people are imaginative liars and can fill in the blanks of details on the spot, and some people cannot. This was all to find out if Emily was able to create details like the ones she had in the story on the fly, and she was failing miserably. However, Brenda didn't discount the fact that a very good con artist would realize this fact, and act accordingly, which was exactly how Emily was acting now.

"No, they wanted to, and they asked me if I wanted to go, but I told them no, that I didn't want to be found. They seemed to understand. They told me, "That's who lives in Canada, people who don't want to be found." Emily managed a weak smile, but again it wasn't returned.

"What about the rest of your time? Were you in the same spot, the same house for the entire time you were missing?"

"Yes, until the rescue workers arrived. We could hear the choppers out in the forest, and I ran after the helicopters, trying to catch them. They were doing low sweeps along the forest, looking for me. I had to run for about half an hour in the direction they were, and it seemed every time I got close to them, they just flew farther away until I finally caught up with them."

"Yes but why did you even need a rescue helicopter? Why didn't you just have your friends bring you back into town or call someone to let them know that's where you were?"

Emily was FUMING at this point. She was mad she had given this interview to Brenda. She was mad that she was told the true story. She decided to make Brenda think it was all a hoax. Brenda wasn't going to be any help, and if she DID believe the story, she was going to go tromping through the Canadian wilderness with a camera crew and a row of trucks, all loaded with gear for kidnapping Bigfoot.

"Because that's where the U.F.O.'s were going to land, and I couldn't let the helicopters land where the U.F.O.s were. You see, the U.F.O.'s are invisible, and I can see them, but nobody else can. I could tell the helicopter pilot couldn't see them either, so I had to run and get his attention before he landed on top of the invisible U.F.O.'s. That's why I didn't have any pants on."

Both Brenda's and Brian's mouths fell open to the floor. Ooooooh-kaaaaaayyyyyy, it was time to go home. Brenda stared at Emily for a second, trying to decide if this was a trick or if she was as insane as she thought. She was definitely smart enough to do something like this to throw Brenda off, but also to make sure no one would waste any time on her, searching for when she was just a lost and confused mental patient.

"Did you get a look at these U.F.O.'s, or were they too far up in the sky to get a good look at to make sure they weren't just airplanes?" Brenda asked slowly, not sure what Emily's next move was going to be.

"Of course I could see them, I just told you. Why don't you ever listen to me? Whenever I give orders around here, no one listens. They're the lizard people, who have come back to reap the planet they planted full of resources two million years ago. WE are their greatest resource. Did you know that over SEVENTEEN BILLION people go missing EVERY YEAR on planet earth, and there is a phone line you can report these missing people to? They've disguised it as a suicide prevention hotline, but I know they're there. I call them up every morning and ask why they want to talk to people who are about to kill themselves. It's so they can be HARVESTED, you know that, right? If it were something else, the government would let the people back to living in the trees, but since we don't WANT to live in the trees, we had to think of something else, didn't we? That something else is the harvesting, which happens every year. All that footage we see on television of people in China and Brazil and Mexico? Doesn't anyone else notice they show the SAME FOOTAGE every year? They want us to think those people are still on earth but they're not! They're on Venus, as slaves! That's what will happen to all of us if we don't stop them! Do you have any chocolate?"

Emily looked at Brenda so sweetly, as if she were a little girl asking for some Halloween candy.

"Allll right and thank you for that. Emily Wrennington, back from being lost in the Canadian wilderness for a month. We're glad to have you home, Emily. This has been Brenda Nova in Quebec, Canada." And with that, the camera light went off.

CHAPTER TWENTY

Brenda stared at Emily, who only gave her a mischievous grin, and a few seconds later, Brenda cracked a HUGE smile along with her. She was BRILLIANT! Brenda couldn't have thought of a better way for her to solve BOTH of their problems at once. First of all, it gave the story enough insanity that it was IMPOSSIBLE to believe. Second, by making herself look like a psychopath, she was let off the hook for any story she gave to the police. Crazy people disappear all the time, and they wouldn't want to waste time and resources on a woman's story who was so obviously out of her mind. If Emily was telling the truth about her friends, she would keep that secret to herself unless she wanted to prove it to Brenda, and it if was bullshit, well, she just covered for herself magnificently. Either way they were both off the hook, giving Brenda an excuse not to follow up, the police a reason not to go looking for an abductor, and Emily a reason to be shown on video without any question as to her credibility; she was obviously out of her mind, and no one would ask any more questions.

"How was that?" Emily asked, still full of pride at her quick thinking.

"I gotta say, that was pretty brilliant. Can I buy you a drink?"

"You can buy me TWO!" pretty Emily said, jumping up in her chair and throwing her jacket on.

As they sat in the bar contemplating the events of the last day, they were all happy to be plied with spirits, each for their own reason.

"I don't think I would have liked Los Angeles anyway" Emily was still testing the waters even though she had made up her mind. "Besides, I would have ruined the careers of all of those actresses when those directors saw me and wanted me in every picture they made."

"Is THAT right?" Brenda was glowing at Emily's transformation to faux streetwise bad girl. Emily loved playing the part, and since this was a town Brenda wouldn't be recognized in, the two girls snuggled up in a gay bar that they found on Google maps. Brian kept getting hit on by every local guy who had been with every other local guy there a dozen times or more, but kept totally focused on the prize- if he could get the two of them back to the hotel drunk enough, or just horny, he was going to have a majestic night.

"Tell me about the craziest sex you've ever had", Emily asked of Brenda, who kept ordering shots.

"The craziest? Well, Brian here is a good solid foundation for some crazy nights, but I wouldn't call them weird. Solid and crazy, but not weird." Brenda ran her hand under the table and found Brian rock hard, to which she guided Emily's hand under the table and let her feel up her camera crew, which Emily and Brian both thoroughly enjoyed. "I think that's a conversation for another night. I'm not drunk enough for that kind of talk, plus, then we'll start to make dares once we get up to the room, and there just isn't enough lumber in that room for that kind of activity, nor am I sure my insurance will cover international hotel repairs. Domestic, definitely, but ……"

"Is THAT right?" Emily repeated, still feeling Brian up. "Well, after I get you some proof you're going to want to come back, hmm? So I can take my time and prepare something special, yes?"

The way she said 'yeeess?' reminded Brenda of an evil scientist from a 60's cartoon. She was totally entranced by Emily once again, and anxious to get back to the room and give both of them a tongue bath.

"Hey Emily want to know what Brian's good at?" and whispered in Emily's ear, to which she glowed like a schoolgirl and blushed, letting her eyes flirt with him. Brian was DYING to know what Brenda was telling Emily, but didn't really care at the same time because he KNEW they were going to turn into a sweaty pile of limbs in about thirty minutes.

Fifteen minutes later, they were back at the hotel, laughing and trying to get the key in right in their drunken state. They didn't exactly have a W in Northern Quebec, but they had a Holiday Inn Executive Suites, which was clean and orderly. Honestly they didn't care, though Brenda would have liked to show Emily some star power. They tumbled into the room and almost instantly Emily asked, "So are you two, like, am I going to get into trouble, or is there a line I shouldn't be crossing, or…."

"Oh, god, go ahead and fuck him! I want to watch!" Emily was thrilled at the reply, and started kissing Brian passionately and trying to hold herself up at the same time. Brian tore at his clothes, Emily at hers, but it seemed Brian had two sets of hands because he managed to get undressed while fondling Emily's breasts at the same time. Brenda noticed that and was actually really impressed and wondered if he did the same thing with her. Brian lifted up her skirt and placed her on the bed, tearing off her brand new black underwear that Brenda had given her, which she very much wanted to keep as a small token. It seemed that Brian and Brenda had the same idea, because the both reached for them as soon as they were off Emily's ass. Brian decided not to fight over them because he had the real thing right in front of him, and decided first he wanted to know what Emily's pussy tasted like. He bent over her on the bed, still half out of his clothes with her underneath him, her legs spread far and looking great in heels and a black skirt hiked up around her waist.

He kissed her thighs gently, making her smile and look over at Brenda, who was reaching inside of her blouse and rubbing her breasts, licking her lips and already wanting to be sandwiched between them. Brian grinned at her, and lifted up Emily's thighs so they were over his shoulders while he lay face down on the bed. He drove his tongue into her fast enough to make her gasp and writhe against the sheets in pleasure, twisting her hips and closing her eyes to get the best effect. Brian was great at something he loved as much as this, and having Emily's sweet hot sex under his face was something he had been dreaming about since he first saw her picture on the telex program. He pulled her pussy lips inside of his mouth and sucked the juice out of her, licking her up and down while seemingly trying to get the whole of her sex in his mouth. Emily's shirt was up above her tits, and she was squeezing them and rubbing her nipples, begging to have Brenda come over and torture and punish her.

Emily opened up her eyes and saw Brenda on the opposite bed with her legs spread wide open, one finger rubbing her shaved pussy up and down, the other inside of her decorative black lace bra, feeling her breasts get bigger the more turned on she got. Brenda's tits were perfect for news casting, and millions of men every day dreamed about licking her luscious breasts for the thirty seconds of her report, longer if it was an interview. The dirty letters she got sometimes turned her on, though she'd never tell anyone that. Emily and Brenda stared at each other for a second, and while Brian kept licking Emily and tongue fucking her, Brenda couldn't take it anymore and climbed on top of Emily.

Brenda let her swollen tits fall out of her bra, unsnapping it in the back in one swift motion and letting them fall on Emily's face. Emily took them in her mouth and made "MMMMmmmmm" sounds as she sucked Brenda's nipples to get them really wet. She took them and rubbed the tips against her own, which were pressed up and held in place by the tightness of her sweater. Brenda soon relieved her of that, and all that remained on Emily's hot young body was the black skirt around her waist. Brian took the cue and pulled it down over her legs and stopped to watch she and Brenda kissing, which is a magical thing for a man to witness.

Soon Brian had the rest of his clothes off as well, and Brenda unbuttoned her blouse and Emily helped her out of her skirt but Brenda left her white panties on, they looked too nice on her tan skin. Emily ran her hand over the soft fabric, and Brenda's swollen pussy lips protruded through the softness of them and made her look like a supermodel in Playboy. While Brian admired the two of them kissing and finishing getting undressed, he toyed with his dick, feeling its smoothness and the stretchiness of the skin over his balls.

"Bring it up here" Brenda asked sweetly, and Brian could hardly wait to comply. He stood on his knees with his cock sticking out at a ninety-degree angle while Brenda pointed it at Emily's mouth. Emily just smiled and took it all in, licking the shaft and sucking on the tip, then tilting her head back and swallowing all of it down her throat.

Brian was hard as a rock and Emily got her saliva all over him, making it glisten in the dim light, but Brenda though it looked wonderful as it ran full bore in and out of Emily's mouth. Brenda had seen Brian's dick a hundred times before and for some reason it looked bigger, more swollen than usual, but she thought maybe because Emily was a little less curvy than she was and it looked bigger by comparison. Brian certainly felt huge, and the motion he and Emily had was making him want to come so badly... He had wanted this for so long, and now he had to try and pace himself. Emily took his balls in her hand and cupped them gently, still swallowing his dick whole and getting her face fucked like the bad girl she wanted to be treated like.

Brenda traded places with her, getting on her knees in front of Brian and stuffing her face full of his cock, tasting Emily's saliva all over it and loving the feeling of it in her mouth. The thought of getting savagely gang banged by a group of man like wild creatures was playing over and over in her mind, and her pussy was tingling and getting wetter as she kept thinking about Emily's story. She knew better than to bring it up. She didn't want Emily getting distracted from servicing Brian the way she was. Emily had squeezed under Brenda to get access to her tits and feel her soft skin on top of her, loving being underneath her and having those giant breasts bouncing back and forth over her face, licking and sucking them each time they came around.

Emily decided to get creative and moved her face under Brenda's pussy, so Emily was on her back with her feet against the headboard, Brenda was on top of her facing Brian on all fours still taking his cock in her mouth, and Brian was up on his knees facing the headboard with his hands on his back hips, feeling the smoothness of his ass and loving the way Brenda's mouth perfectly circled around his dick when she sucked on it. Emily was ferociously licking Brenda's pussy, feeling the softness of her freshly shaved labia and getting tickled in her nose as Brenda's pubic mound moved over her face.

Brian pulled out of Brenda's mouth, and just said, "I can't TAKE it anymore. I HAVE to come. We'll fuck more later, I promise." Brenda knew he was good for it, and let him flip her over as he drove his cock into her pussy HARD. She lay on her back while Brian hammered away at her, both of them moaning and loving the feeling of their mutually beneficial friendship, and Emily lay beside

Brenda getting fingered and rubbing her tits together on Brenda's face. Brian really couldn't stand the sight of them together, it was driving him completely insane with lust, and he fucked Brenda's pussy for all he was worth, already feeling the come ripping out of his dick before he even felt like he was peaking. He knew it was going to be a good, hot, long orgasm, and he wanted to enjoy every second of it. He grabbed both of their tits and drowned his face in them, sucking and licking at all four of them, hammering Brenda and getting the full effect of having two girls under him.

He pulled out of Brenda and shoved himself into Emily, who moaned "OOOOHHHHHHHH!!!" and fucked her as hard as he could. He was still building up and still spraying his load inside of her, knowing nothing could stop it now, and loving every second of it. He ADORED having these gorgeous females underneath him, licking each others' faces and grabbing both of their tits as they bounced and rubbed together with his fucking motion, and the come kept spraying out of him and now he was yelling "UUUNH!! UUUHHHHHHH!!!" and SQUEEZING those GORGEOUS tits with everything he had, DYING to spray a whole load of cum all over their pretty little faces, their red swollen ruby lips, he kept his eyes open saying, "LET ME SEE YOUR TONGUE! SHOW ME WHERE YOU WANT ME TO COME!!!" and both girls daintily opened their mouths and let their tongues slide all over each other, sending him further over the edge, squeezing their tits, and with a final "OOOOOOOHHHHHHHH!!!!!" he pulled out of Emily, who had been bucking WILDLY with her tongue sticking out of her face licking Brenda, and pointed his dick at both of their faces, shooting his hot load all over their open mouths, their swollen red lips and those hot wet tongues as the girls licked it all over each others' faces, licking the tip of his dick while he came and tightened up his whole body with excitement, Brenda pulling his dick closer and swallowing as much as she could then holding his tip with her tongue against Emily's face, watching the last of it shoot over her cheeks and mouth while she licked it up and swallowed every last drop she could suck out of it.

Brian sat motionless on the bed, still frozen with Emily's tits squeezed in one hand and his cock in the other, now with his eyes closed and his dick frozen in Emily's mouth, pulsing and throbbing with the last of his explosion. Emily knew what she was doing, she swallowed a much as she could, and held it in her mouth, sucking on him but holding still so he could enjoy fucking her face and mouth feeling the last moments of pure pleasure. After a few seconds his body relaxed and he slumped on the bed, looking as if he had just undergone electroshock therapy.

"I'm sorry but I couldn't help it. I had to come but I'll take care of you girls now." He was breathing so hard and sweating so badly he wondered how he was going to get up.

"Don't worry about it lover, you just relax. There's no hurry and we've got plenty of room". Brenda was still kissing Emily, licking the white hot come off of her face, and Emily was doing the same. They were tasting each other's mouths, licking and swallowing each other while licking each other clean, still horny and turned on. Brian turned to get a cigarette, and they all shared one for a few minutes.

"Maybe we should bring you back to L.A. with us. If nothing else, you could hang out on the beach for a few days, sounds like you could use a vacation."

"Tell you what. If you guys give me a place to stay, I'll pay for my own ticket. I never said I was poor." Brenda smiled at this idea. She was hesitant to ask Mel for a ticket when she wasn't sure if there was anything that they were going to sell to the media outlets from the interview, and she knew Mel wasn't going to want to pay for a ticket after an interview like that. As if on cue, the phone rang.

Giggling, Brenda grabbed the phone and put it on the bed before picking up the receiver.

"MMMmmmhhhhello? Oh, HI Mel! Yeah, we were just thinking about you! Really? You know, working hard. Oh you can tell huh? How can you tell that?"

After three more seconds her face froze. She sat totally motionless for a few seconds and then looked at Brian with the face of death, her mouth open and her eyes as big as saucers. Something was very, very, VERY wrong.

"Oh, I see...and ....Okay. Yeah. Okay."

She listened for another thirty seconds all the time staring at Brian, her mouth open. Something had happened. All of the joy had been sucked out of the room and was replaced with a big black cloud.

"Okay. Yes, yes sir. All right."

She hung up the phone. "We have to leave for Los Angeles right now. Emily, we'll have to bring you out another time. I'm so sorry we have to cut our night short, but Brian and I have to be on a plane for Japan in the morning, and we have to charter a jet to be out of her in an hour.

"Is everything all right?"

"Yes honey, everything's okay as far as you're concerned. But I'm so sorry but we have to cut our evening short. Do you need cab fare? (Translation: get the fuck out)

"No, I'm okay". Emily was already getting dressed. Sometimes when you feel that the party's over, you don't want to be in the room anymore. Something had happened, and they weren't going to tell Emily what it was. Emily wasn't even sure Brian knew the way he looked at her, but he was a professional and knew better than to ask in front of Emily. If it concerned her, Brenda would have told her. Emily buttoned and zipped and was out the door in a flash. She gave each of them a quick kiss even though it felt uncomfortable, and after a quick exchange of numbers, she was out the door.

CHAPTER TWENTY-ONE

Brenda turned slowly to look at Brian, who was feeling the seriousness of the situation and putting his pants on.

"You.... sent Mel...the TAPE?!?!?"

The look on Brenda's face was fire. She had NEVER been this pissed at anyone in her LIFE.

"Well,......yeah, I mean...was I not supposed to?"

"YOU...SENT MEL...THE TAPE?!?!?!?"

"Well, actually, I uploaded it, so it was instantaneous, but yeah, why? That chick was out of her MIND with all of that Bigfoot shit!"

"BRIAN, I SPENT THE AFTERNOON FUCKING HER IN THAT ROOM. FUCKING HER. THAT WAS ON THE TAPE ALSO. ALONG WITH THE FACT THAT WE MADE UP A DIFFERENT STORY AND I DIDN'T MENTION THAT THERE WERE GOING TO BE TWO STORIES. BRIAN DO YOU KNOW WHAT YOU HAVE DONE?!?!"

Brian's mouth dropped to the floor

"WHAT DO YOU MEAN YOU SPENT THE AFTERNOON FUCKING HER WHILE THE TAPE WAS ROLLING?!?! ARE YOU OUT OF YOUR MIND?!?! BRENDA SHE WAS OUR STORY, NOT YOUR LITTLE PLAYTHING!! WHY THE FUCK DIDN'T YOU SAY SOMETHING TO ME?!?! I ASKED YOU IF

I SHOULD REMOVE THE TAPE AND YOU SAID NO YOU COULD HAVE SAID SOMETHING THEN!!!!"

"WELL I DIDN'T THINK YOU WERE GOING TO UPLOAD IT UNTIL WE DECIDED!!!"

"BRENDA, IT'S NOT UP TO US WHAT TO PUT ON THE NEWS!!! ONCE EMILY SIGNED THAT PAPER, EVERYTHING SHE SAYS BECOMES PROPERTY OF THE MEDIA CENTER INCLUDING YOUR LITTLE INTERLUDE!!!"

"BUT AT THE BEGINNING SHE SAID THAT SHE WANTED US TO HELP HER! WHEN DID YOU SEND IT?!?!"

"I SENT IT AFTER I GRABBED THE CAMERA! I THOUGHT YOU WANTED IT UPLOADED!!! I THOUGHT IT WAS GOING TO SAVE US SOME TIME SO THEY COULD EDIT IT BACK AT THE STATION WHILE WE GOT A SECOND INTERVIEW!!!! JESUS CHRIST, BRENDA! HOW FUCKING LONG HAVE WE BEEN WORKING TOGETHER?!?! YOU THOUGHT I WAS GOING TO HANG ON TO THAT TAPE UNTIL YOU MADE THE DECISION WHICH VERSION TO AIR?"

"YES!!!!"

"AND YOU FUCKED HER IN THE MIDDLE OF THE INTERVIEW?!?!"

"YES!!!!!"

"OH, SHIT!" Brian was turning as many colors and Brenda was. He wasn't sure if he was going to be a hero around the office when he got back or if he was going to get fired. Brenda felt as if she didn't want to return to Los Angeles at ALL.

"Well what did Mel say? Maybe this isn't so bad. So it's a little embarrassing. You don't think he showed it around the office or anything do you?"

"BRIAN, THOSE UPLOADS DON'T EVEN GO TO HIM! THEY GO FROM THE COM SAT RELAY TO THE EDITING BAY, WHERE EVERYONE I KNOW WORKS! THAT INTERVIEW WAS UP THERE FOR EVERYONE TO SEE AND ohhhhhhh, JESUS, I need to get fucking DRUNK! Mel told me that the tape was unfinished, and did I know there was a taped sex scene with myself and the interviewee in the middle of the interview? I felt like I wanted to DIE. OR KILL YOU."

"Hey, do not, DO NOT, put this on me. YOU KNOW GOD DAMNED WELL that if I CAN, I'll upload whatever we have on tape. I had NO IDEA you didn't want me to. YOU were the one who wanted the camera rolling, and so YOU gave me permission to film. Once it's in the can, it's property of our company. Even BEFORE it's uploaded it's company property. JESUS NOW I gotta send them ANOTHER interview, TOTALLY DIFFERENT...Wait a minute. The new interview was about U.F.O.'s right?"

"Yeah"

"And they think she's just fucking NUTS at the station, right?"

"Yeah"

"So we send them a few bits about U.F.O.'s and your opening and closing statements and identifiers, and they can make whatever they want out of it. Do you really think anyone is going to believe her after she says that Bigfoot and the ALIENS abducted her?"

"Well, no, but...."

"WELL THEN PROBLEM SOLVED! I'LL edit together the parts from the new interview, she looks like a freak, and even if they DO air the parts of Bigfoot on the air, no one is going to believe her, right?"

"I guess not, but they HAVE to air the parts about aliens and U.F.O.s, also, can you call them and make sure they edit that in? I mean if they decide to use it at all?"

"Of course baby. And you know what else, I'll make sure that no one is making copies of your sex scene, okay? I know those guys, and I'm sure they'd tell you they wouldn't do it, but let me ask them. Here's the original copy. "

He handed Brenda a black 3m digital tape cartridge and she put it in her bag. She sniffled a bit and Brian was surprised to see her crying.

"Come on, it's not that bad. I'll call everyone now and do damage control. Everyone worships you there anyway, so they see you having sex, big deal. It'll add a little excitement to their lives for a minute. Even if word gets around the office it'll only stay a rumor if you let it upset you. If you show them you don't care, that you're comfortable with it, that you're not ashamed of being sexy, then it'll make you an even bigger legend than you are. Now that's not so bad, is it?"

This was a girl he had seen take on heads of state, walk over presidents and ex presidents, spit on sexist protocol for visiting dignitaries, and she was getting upset over her body exposed He told her exactly what he had just thought, and she sniffled and smiled a little and curled in his arms. Brian got on the phone, and after some very delicate conversations, asked who knew and whom they had told. Then he called THOSE people and seemed to nip it in the bud. He even called a few extra people just to see of they had heard any rumors going around about Brenda or anyone else and no, they hadn't, or had already been told to shut up about it.

That night Brenda lay in Brian's arms and was thankful for him once again. Every girl should have a Brian, she thought to herself, snuggling in his neck, and kissing him to sleep, not before he went down on her and made her come like a racehorse, but even if it was to relieve the stress of her day, he was a champ. The next day they walked into the office all smiles as if nothing was wrong, Canada was a party! Whoo! Those Canadians! Brian played it up too but did NOT mention that he had sex with their interview subject. They edited the piece together so it read, "Girl rescued after being abducted by Bigfoot; aliens" and they aired ten seconds of her talking about flying saucers. She mentioned Bigfoot once.

The next morning they were on a plane to Japan. They spent the week at a posh hotel, and Brenda was back in her element amongst foreign dignitaries, diplomats, and five star services. She had her Brian with her, so she felt safe and secure, even as the Japanese high counselors hit on her and asked her for dates while in town. It was kind of expected, and the Japanese are the type who feel that if you don't ask to take someone out on the town, that's rude. They ate wonderful food, met amazing people, and had great sex in the hotel afterwards.

When they got back ten days later, there was a message from Emily. Brenda thought she wanted to thank her for keeping her story looking too insane to be followed up on. They did such a good job of it in editing, that no one, not for a SECOND, did anyone even ask, "Is she being for real?" Brenda sat at her desk and dialed her number, and after a few rings she picked up.

"Brenda?"

"Hey darling! How they treating you in Canada?"

"Well, our little plan seemed to work, they quit asking me about where I was after the story aired, but that's not why I'm calling."

"What's up?"

"How would you like the story of your career served to you on a silver platter?"

"Only if you'll be my girlfriend", Brenda flirted with her.

"I'm serious"

"Not with the bigfoot again, I can only do that once a year."

"It's bigger than that"

"Aliens?"

"Brenda"

"Yeah?"

"............"

"Emily?"

"............"

"Emily are you okay?"

"...............Look in your text message inbox"

Brenda swiped her smartphone screen over just as a text message with an attachment arrived. She clicked on it and waited a few seconds while the 'downloading' prompt circled, something she wished the makers of these things would fix so the message AND attachment were waiting for you when you opened the phone. She clicked on the little icon next to 'open or save' and nearly dropped the phone. On her little five inch screen was a perfect image, crystal clear and un-Photoshopped, of Emily looking radiantly beautiful alongside a beast, a giant of a man with reddish brown dark hair all over his (its?) body, including its face, making it look more like Chewbacca than a gorilla, but with decidedly human blue eyes. At their feet was a miniature creature of the same type, looking like a giant teddy bear but sitting up and reaching for Emily, oblivious to what the camera was. She trembled as she put it back up to her ear and asked, "Is that what I think it is?"

"Now remember, you PROMISED if I GOT YOU PROOF, you WOULD NOT say a word to ANYONE, do I still have your promise?"

Brenda was frozen still. All she could do was become Emily's best friend and help with whatever she wanted, hoping that at the end of this rainbow there was going to be Pulitzer prizes, royal biological society dinners, invitations from the president, this could make her bigger than anyone in the world, and to get that, she had to have Emily's confidence.

"You have my word."

"Brenda"

"Yes?"

There was a long silence that weighed heavily in the air. Both of them could feel it. It was thick enough to cut with a knife.

Brenda could hear Emily breathing, the kind of breaths that come when your body hasn't moved an inch but your heart is racing a mile a minute. All she could do was listen, and after about thirty seconds she realized that she hadn't been breathing at all, and turned her mouth away from the phone to sharply inhale. She then heard two words.

"I'm pregnant".

TO BE CONTINUED...................

Printed in Great Britain
by Amazon

17313650R00113